GUARDED STAR

Christine Ashworth

"Ashworth's talent shines…."

—*New York Times* Bestselling Author Maggie Shayne on *Demon Hunt*

MAKE A WISH

Everyone leaves twenty-five-year-old Evie Marcherand, but with her naturally husky voice and musical talent she's done okay, and her star is rising. Her songs and her guitar? *Those* she can count on. She's just booked her first three-city tour. Too bad someone else wants to stop her music. Permanently.

Jake Wells. 39. Private investigator. Tall and lanky, with brown hair that's going silver at his temples. What does he want? To go on vacation. But with four younger sisters, "protective" doesn't *begin* to describe him, so a promise to a dead man means he'll play bodyguard instead. Threats of violence against an up-and-coming singer/songwriter have been escalating, and there's just no way that's going to happen. But after he gets a taste of Evie Marcherand's music—and lips—there's no saying what will.

GUARDED STAR

Christine Ashworth

www.BOROUGHSPUBLISHINGGROUP.com

GUARDED STAR
Copyright © 2015 Christine Ashworth

ISBN 978-1-942886-25-9

To Brenda Chin, who set me on the right path for this story two years ago. Your faith in me came at exactly the right time. Thank you so much.

ACKNOWLEDGMENTS

To Jill Limber, thanks so much for not only bringing me to the Boroughs team, but for being excited at having me here. Working with you, Chris Keeslar and Michelle Klayman has been a joy. My thanks also to copy editor, Tanya Reynolds. You are awesome, my friend.

My thanks also to Roz Lee, who was the first to recognize that Mike's ghost needed to depart the pages, lol. I fought you on that but had to laugh when, six months later, the first words out of Brenda Chin's mouth were, "You need to lose that ghost."

And to my husband, the actor/hippy/guitar/jester guy who loves me beyond anything I had ever expected in life, thank you for your persistent encouragement to do this writing gig. Let's do a few more decades together, shall we?

CONTENTS

GUARDED STAR

CHAPTER ONE

The wake for legendary guitarist Mike Harper rocked the town of Ocean Beach, California. The band, playing in the brightly lit parking lot next to the sand, sent riffs rolling through the hot summer night. Flames leapt high in the fire ring on the sand, and the blacktop roiled with swimsuit-clad fans and neighbors dancing to the beat. The scent of barbecue, baby oil, and burning driftwood perfumed the air.

Evie Marcherand had done her duty as hostess. Now, hours later, she hovered at the firelight's edge, the cheerful crowd unable to fill the hole in her heart. When Mike died, so did her security. He'd been the father she didn't have. Teacher, mentor, friend, Mike had also been her salvation and her anchor.

Dealing with the aftermath of his death the past few weeks had kept her busy. The band and their families, bless them, had rallied around, keeping her occupied and laughing as they boxed up Mike's clothes and photos—sending the first to charity, and the second to his ex-wives. So it wasn't until now, with nothing left to do, that grief threatened to tear her chest wide open.

She hung in limbo tonight. Her life with Mike was over, and her life as a singer/songwriter wouldn't start in earnest until tomorrow. Distraction, that's what she needed. Something to get her from tonight's limbo to tomorrow's hectic schedule. She nodded to a hired cop, bent to grab a beer—one of the perks of having a special permit for the party—and pulled the tab on the can. The ocean beckoned and a full moon shone bright overhead, providing plenty of light. She headed away from the crowd and into the night, toward the rolling waves, the white foam sparkling in the moonlight.

Tomorrow she'd be talking to her new manager about her career. Tomorrow she'd honor her promise to Mike and spread her fledgling wings in the music industry. For the first time ever, starting tomorrow she'd live life on her own terms. Put her needs and desires first, instead of putting Mike first. Mike, who no longer needed her companionship or nursing care.

She pushed the painful thought away and focused on the future. In a couple of days, she'd start her first-ever very short tour. The

10

tour she'd thought was at least two months away had been moved up, and she was equal parts thrilled and scared to death.

It took her breath away, the possibilities, and yet it also weighed heavily on her mind. Sent her heart racing. Suddenly she felt fifteen again, homeless, and scared about her future. To calm her nerves, she stared out over the ocean as she walked in the light of the moon, letting the sound of the waves soothe her ragged soul.

***

Jake Wells hadn't been near waves after sunset in years, having learned to prefer the ocean under the glare of noon. Moonlit summer beaches were not his style. Yet here he was, heading to a wake straight from a client meeting and getting sand in his dress shoes, all because of a promise to a dead man.

While he doubted Mike's protégé, the young Evie, would actually be at the event, he could at least check out the band, the people she spent time with, see what's what. The invitation indicated hot women, cold beer, and food. If he were ten years younger, he'd dive in, no problem. But now, only his sense of duty held him there. His promise to Mike.

The changed touring dates meant he'd had to postpone his vacation to France and Spain. Pushing his vacation back a week wasn't too bad, all things considered.

Jake loosened his tie and stopped a couple hundred feet from the party. The moonlight made it easy to see, and the lights from the parking lot shone down on the dancing crowd. Still undecided about joining the party, he saw the woman before she saw him as she wandered across the sand away from the firelight, alone and looking none too steady on her feet.

He stifled a sigh. *Beach* plus *moonlight* plus *woman* equaled *trouble*, his divorce the living proof of that equation. Still, his protective streak, stronger than ever after seeing his four younger sisters safely navigate their teens and twenties, had him moving toward her. The sooner she went back to the bonfire and safety, the sooner he could leave.

As he closed the distance between them, the visual impact of her stole his breath.

She glowed in the moonlight, an ethereal sight, her slender curves pale against an electric blue bikini, short blonde hair a nimbus curling around her head. She clutched a can of beer in one hand and her gaze remained fixed on the waves. She came closer, almost within touching distance.

He took another, involuntary, step toward her. "Hey there. The party's the other way."

She stumbled at his words. Quicker than thought he was there to steady her, his hands on her shoulders. Shock zipped through him. He heard her sharp intake of breath. Her skin felt like warm silk, tempting him to stroke. He snatched his hands away and repressed the curses that rose to his lips. Time seemed to stretch.

"You startled me." Dark eyes met his and widened before she dropped her gaze. "I know where the party is." Her voice, caramel over smoke, slid into his gut as sweetly as any honed knife. "I'm escaping," she confided. She made a move to go around him.

He couldn't help himself. He reached out and closed his hand gently around her upper arm. "Stay." Jake frowned down at her blonde head. She was such a tiny thing. "I mean, you should stay near the bonfire. Walking at night on the beach isn't the smartest thing to do."

She shot him a measuring look. "I'm quite capable of taking care of myself," she said. "And it *is* a public beach." She hesitated, looking to the horizon. Sighed. "You're right, though. Running away won't solve anything." A thread of sadness ran through her words, hooking him deep.

"You came from the wake." He released her reluctantly and shoved his hands in his pockets. "How's the food?"

"Good. There's plenty. And everyone's done crying, so they're in party mode at this point. Were you on your way there?" She looked him up and down, a smile tugging at her full lips. "Not exactly dressed for it, are you, in suit and tie? Did you know Mike well?" She cocked her head up at him, and Jake finally got to see the rest of her face. Short blonde curls floated around high cheekbones. Her eyes were filled with pain. She was older than he'd first thought. Early twenties was his guess.

Even as he took stock of her, those eyes changed, the pain layered with curiosity, darkening with knowledge as their gazes locked. "No," she said slowly, "you didn't know Mike. Somehow, I think I would have remembered you." Her voice grew even huskier.

Her face tilted up to his, she licked her lips and took a swaying step forward. "I came this way looking for a distraction," she murmured. "I guess you're it. It's been a while, but you never forget some things."

His mouth dried as she took another step forward, her sensuality scrambling his wits. "Distraction?" He caught her by the shoulders. His fingers caressed the silky skin even as he considered his sanity. "Distraction from what?"

The waves rushed to the shore with a froth of sound. The moon shone down on them, and music drifted up the beach from the party. It seemed an eternity between his question and her answer.

She shrugged easily in his hold. "Wakes. The future. Death. Take your pick." One of her hands settled firmly at his waist, underneath his suit jacket, sending new heat sizzling through him. "Distractions are good. Keep the pain at bay, right? And as distractions go, you're a doozy."

Jake's head spun. Her scent rose between them, something light, delicate, and utterly feminine.

"Surely you have something you need distracting from? Someone?" She took a step closer and the beer in her hand pressed against his side, cold through his shirt. A breath separated their bodies.

He held her away from him, took a step back and hauled in air. "Little girls shouldn't play with fire." He fought the urge to give in to her heat, unable to tear his gaze from her.

"Sometimes that's the only way to get warm," she murmured, and she smiled at him. Her tongue teased him as she swiped her full bottom lip.

That was all it took. Jake's usually rock-solid control snapped and he swooped. His lips found hers and took. And even as he did, he cursed the night and the moonlight and the magic on the beach.

The woman in his arms rose up to soothe him, and the anger that had come out of nowhere drained away. He gathered her closer, her silken skin warm beneath his hands, urging him to take even more. Her free hand dug into his hair, held on tight as her lips opened, inviting him in, her actions focusing his attention.

Jake found his hold gentling even as their kiss changed. Deepened. Slid him straight into a fantasy world, something so new, so unlike anything he'd ever felt before, that need mixed with curiosity held him there under the moonlight. The spice of her seduced him, kept him wanting more.

She tasted of tears and joy. Of confusion and laughter and wonder. His world narrowed down to simply her, the feel of her, soft and warm in his arms. Her taste made him yearn. His entire world spun off course because of that kiss.

It wasn't until she lowered her heels into the sand and eased her mouth away from his with a last nip at his bottom lip that he struggled to calm his racing heart. He did his best to remember to breathe, even as her hand, trailing down his chest, threatened to take breath from him again. She took a small step back.

"You're almost too much of a distraction." She looked up at him with a rueful smile and winked. "Here. Take my beer. I haven't had any of it, and I don't really want it."

Jake took the beer from her, watched as she took another step back, seemingly unaffected by what they had just shared. "Where are you going?" How could she leave? How could he let her leave? Adrenaline coursed through him.

She cast a look over her shoulder to where the party still rocked. "I need to get back. Come find me at the bonfire. Maybe we can pick up where we left off? Because I'd really like that." She blew him a sassy kiss as she backed away. "Thanks. That was one hell of a— distraction." She turned then and walked back to the crowd.

Jake watched those slender hips sway with the effort of walking on sand, and he tipped the beer down his dry throat, locking his knees. He would not go after her.

In spite of her invitation, running after her would look ridiculous, and he had his pride. Better, by far, to let her go. Consign her memory to "what might have been," a rare fantasy for a man who worked hard. Tomorrow he started a new job, and that's where his mind needed to be.

He frowned. Not going to the bonfire meant he couldn't find out about Mike's protégé. But if he did go, and met up with the whiskey-voiced pixie instead, he wouldn't be thinking about work. Well, hell. He'd meet his client tomorrow then, at the talent manager's office, what was his name? Conway Davis. StarTide Agency.

He gave the bonfire, and the dancing crowd, one last look. Sometimes being the responsible one really sucked.

Draining the beer, he tossed the empty can into a trashcan emblazoned with "Keep San Diego's Beaches Clean" and headed to his car, to his apartment, and to an undoubtedly sleepless night.

CHAPTER TWO

"I've got you booked in Vegas for three shows on two nights, then in Scottsdale for two nights, and in Los Angeles for one night with a possible holdover for a second night. They might have a cancellation, and if you do well the first night they may have you stay for another one." Conway cast an irritated glance at the closed office door. "My secretary should have left the itinerary here somewhere. She was supposed to make copies yesterday, but she's new."

"Another one? You go through secretaries like water," Evie said, and laughed. "At least, Mike was always saying you liked them tall, busty, and brainless." Conway Davis was blond, a younger and more toothsome version of Matthew McConaughey. He was also about as deep as a child's plastic wading pool, according to Mike. Evie had yet to make up her mind on that point.

He grinned. "So I like eye candy. Sue me. It won't stop the StarTide Agency from getting you awesome contracts."

"The agency should get a secretary who can actually file. Just saying." Evie refrained from rolling her eyes even as her stomach lurched. Conway didn't have to take her on as a client. She knew it was Mike again, working his magic even after his death. She took a calming breath. "Are we done here?"

"Almost. We need to talk about your entourage," he said, glancing again at the door. "You know the band. They have their own tour bus, and Mike, of course, has given you his." He looked down at his desk, shuffled some papers there.

"Of course?" Another shock. She shook her head. "What do you mean, of course? There was nothing in the will about his tour bus."

Conway gave her his signature grin-and-wink. "Oh, I know. He signed the title over when he signed the house over to you, almost a year ago, to avoid any messy tax issues. He wanted me to wait until he was gone before I told you. It's all taken care of, all in your name. You've even been paying insurance and DMV fees on it."

"I have?" Her mind whirled. She still hadn't gotten over the news about the dear little beach house being hers, along with a checking account to help with its upkeep. Now with the bus, she felt overwhelmed. "I'm not used to owning stuff." She thought about the clothes shopping Mike made her do and squirmed inside. "Too much stuff. Besides, I don't have the money to put gas in the thing," she protested, panic threatening. "What am I going to do with a tour bus?"

"Enjoy it. Or sell it. Up to you."

Evie froze. The words came from the doorway behind her, but it was that voice that had her forgetting to breathe. She'd spent a restless night haunted by the kiss she'd provoked in the moonlight. She stood and turned and there he was, in a white shirt, dark suit, and impeccably tied deep blue tie, with dark sunglasses shading his eyes. Before she could say a word, Conway was at the door greeting their guest.

"You're late. But I'm glad you're here. Come in."

Evie watched his every move, her body heating up in memory. Beneath the suit was a fit man, one that moved with confidence and grace.

Her hands had touched his broad chest, clung around his neck during their kiss on the moonlit beach. Wanted to strip him.

She'd had a surprisingly difficult time stepping back from him and walking away. Man oh man, what a kiss.

His dark hair, with a hint of silver at the temples, flopped over his forehead and curled to below his collar, giving him a raffish look. She remembered the silky softness of his hair, and her fingers ached to dive in again. But she was most curious about his eyes. She hadn't seen his eyes last night, not really. She held her breath until he sat, removed his shades, and turned to send her a cautious look.

Blue. They were blue, almost navy so blue. The same color as his tie. Her gaze dropped to his lips, now quirked in a sudden smile. A slight tremor ran through her body.

"Evie, I'd like to introduce you to Jake Wells. Jake, Evie Marcherand."

Jake nodded. "A pleasure."

She raised a brow. "Likewise. What are you doing here?" Her pulse kicked into high gear.

A smile flickered at the corner of his mouth. "Your bodyguard. At your service."

Her mouth fell open. "No fucking way. Con?" She turned to her agent. "Bodyguard? He can't be serious."

"Yes, bodyguard. He'll be on the bus with you. Would anyone like coffee? No? I'll be right back," and Conway slipped out of the office, shutting the door behind him.

"Coward," she muttered, turning her attention back to Jake. In the moonlight, he'd stolen her breath with the touch of his lips, the care she felt in his arms. In daylight, he was even more devastating. She noted the black eyebrows over those amazing eyes, the cheekbones that hinted at maybe Native American blood. The thin, mobile lips that had worked magic on hers.

"How old are you?" The words sounded jerked from Jake's mouth.

"Twenty-five. You?" She tilted her head, finally meeting his gaze.

"Thirty-nine." His answer was clipped, his eyes guarded.

Her eyebrows rose. "Interesting." Damn. "I appreciate your visit, but I don't need a bodyguard. You may go." She forced herself to turn away, cross her legs and fold her hands in her lap. The skirt and heels was not her usual outfit, but she felt the occasion deserved getting dressed up some. Now she wished she were in jeans and tennis shoes—the better to run. She stared at Conway's desk and wished desperately that Jake would just go away.

She heard him sigh and stand. She closed her eyes in relief. Or was that disappointment? But instead of hearing the door open, she felt the warmth of him surround her, breathed in the remembered scent of him. A sudden craving for his kiss made her mouth water.

She opened her eyes to find him hovering over her, his hands on the arms of her chair, enclosing the two of them. He studied her, taking his time, and when his gaze dropped to her mouth her tongue gave a nervous swipe of her bottom lip. The same move that caused him to lose control the night before. Today it seemed he was immune to her.

What a shame. It had been so long since anyone had spoken her physical language. The kiss they'd shared told her he not only spoke it, but was fluent.

His voice was low, husky. "No one dismisses me. Especially after I've been hired."

Without thinking too much about it, she touched his cheek, skimmed a finger along his jaw, outlined his lips. Found herself softening on the whole bodyguard thing. "I'm sorry. But you're not coming with me."

Impatience came and went across his face. "You don't have a choice, Evie. Mike hired me to keep you safe. Just like he set up the tour, he set you up with me. I'm yours, your bodyguard, your lifeline."

"Mike hired you? He hired you for *me*?" Mentally she reeled as, that fast, her objections to having a bodyguard came back. "When? To be what, a surrogate daddy? I don't need another one. Mike was more than I deserved."

Jake straightened, stepped back and sat on the edge of Conway's desk. "As to the when, he contacted me two months ago. We had lunch. Just before his last decline. I'm pretty sure he didn't hire me as a surrogate, uh, daddy."

She glared. "For how long?"

"What?"

Evie waved in impatience. "How long did he hire you for? Just the tour?" She watched as wariness crept into his gaze.

"For starters," he said. "Does it matter?"

"Yes, it matters." She jumped up and walked to the window, stared out at the quiet streets. This part of downtown San Diego didn't see much action on a Saturday. "I feel like a package he's given to you to babysit." Emotion balled up in her stomach. "I don't understand. It's ridiculous. Overboard, just like the motorhome. Why did he bother?"

"He loved you." The words were spoken simply, with no extra flourish or explanation.

Evie's heart hitched and tears stung her eyes. She blinked hard. "That's it?" The words caught in her throat, but he heard her.

"That's everything. People do the strangest things out of love."

"Mike gave you me. Or gave me you." She turned and looked at him, a helpless feeling coursing through her, dampening her innate desire to jump his bones. Sexy, yeah, but right now it was his take on her world that she needed. "Is that, you know, normal?"

"Was anything about Mike normal?" With the quirk of an eyebrow and an easy smile, Jake shrugged. "It's my first time being given to someone else. I promise I will keep you safe. Besides, all the stars have bodyguards."

"It's not like I'm a star. I'm bottom rung. I can't see why I need you hanging around. Unless you're planning on getting me food when I want it, or will run errands, like picking up my dry cleaning," she goaded. "You could be my personal—no, slave isn't the right word…concierge, maybe? Yeah. I think I like that."

Jake crossed his arms, looking stiff and uncomfortable. "Mike's reasons were his own." There was an edge to his voice. "Do you really want me to say, ah, he was just a sick, sick man and didn't know that he was spending his money unwisely? Mike was smart. He knew what he was doing. The services I provide don't come cheap. And Mike's already paid me. Instead of acting like a child, you might try being a bit grateful for his forethought."

Evie felt the blood drain from her face. She looked down at her shoes and wished again, rather desperately, for running shoes and a pair of jeans.

"Of course I'm grateful. I just don't understand. And I'm bottom rung. Period," she reiterated, and winced at the panic she heard in her voice.

There was a pause. Evie refused to look at Jake, but she heard his long, slow intake of breath. As if he was being careful about the words that would come out next. Her nerves strung tight, she waited for him to speak.

He let out his breath. "Are you bottom rung? Perhaps. Currently. But from what Mike said, you won't stay at the bottom for long, and now is the time for protection. Which reminds me. Before Conway comes back in, I want to ask you a question."

Evie cocked her head to one side. "What?" The attraction was back on top, sliding through her like a fever. Damn. If he's really going to be her bodyguard, she'll have a serious time keeping her hands off him.

"When you said you were sorry, were you talking about firing me? Or about the kiss we shared last night?" His voice deepened as he spoke.

The finest shiver spread across Evie's body and she spoke without thinking. "I was not apologizing for the kiss. In fact, perhaps having you guard my body might be" she caught her breath, licked her bottom lip, "a very good thing."

They locked gazes. "You are not what I expected," he murmured. "Did you and Mike ever? You know."

Evie sent him a glare of shocked disapproval. "Of course not."

A knock came at the door before it opened and Conway peered in. "All okay? Good, no blood," and he took his place behind the desk as Jake resumed his seat.

Evie's brain was in turmoil. How could Jake think what he had thought? What had Mike told Jake about her to make him think that way?

"Now, Evie. You'll have Mike's driver, Rhoads, driving your bus, and his wife, Thelma Lou, riding with you and Jake. You probably won't see much of them when you aren't on the road. The band, as I said, will be in a separate bus. Bear is in charge of all the logistics at the different venues. You'll be on the road tomorrow morning. Any questions?"

She pulled her mind from the problem of Jake and went swiftly over the details of the tour Mike put together for her. "No, no questions. I'm good. I've got a costume fitting this afternoon, but everything else is solid."

"Well, that's it." Conway stood as she did, reaching across to shake Evie's hand. "I'll catch you at your show in Los Angeles. You're ready, Evie. I know it, and what's more important, Mike knew it, too. It's time."

"Thanks, Con." She squeezed his hand, her stomach queasy. "I should go. Last-minute stuff, you know, plants to water, packing to finish." Nerves to squelch. Antacids to take. She turned toward Jake. "Please don't feel you have to take this job. Conway can figure something out between the two of you, I'm sure." She glanced at Conway. "Right?" It was a last-ditch effort, and everyone in the room knew it.

Conway studied her with concern. "Evie. You know someone had been, uh, bothering Mike, kind of like stalking him, right? He was afraid it might spill over to you. Mike loved you, like the daughter he never had. He wanted to keep you safe this first time out, while you're still getting your feet wet in this industry. I think, for Mike's sake if not your own, that you should accept his gift of a bodyguard with good grace. After this, if you don't want to hire another one, then we'll talk."

Evie swallowed hard. Damn Conway for using Mike as a pressure point. She turned to Jake with a barely concealed sigh. "I'll see you tomorrow, I guess."

He held out a hand and she took it. They stood there for a moment until, with a little flutter deep inside her stomach, she released him. "Bye."

As she walked to the car, for the first time since Mike died Evie felt a lightness of being, a tremor of anticipation just lingering in the air. Maybe having Jake along wouldn't be a bad thing. She remembered their kiss the night before and heat spread through her body. Words filled her mind and a melody haunted her. She grinned as she drove. Her music would see her through this transition. It always did.

**

Jake sent a glare of accusation at Conway as the door closed behind Evie. Damn the man. He had been sure Evie was, at the most, a sixteen-year-old prodigy. Not this quirky, fascinating, wildly alive and amazing woman that he wanted without restraint. It startled him. Scared him.

Con held up his hand and waited until they heard the bell for the elevator ding, signaling Evie's departure. He sat back with a sigh of relief. "Glad that's over with. I thought for sure she was gonna hit the roof."

"That woman is no child." The surprise at finding his fantasy woman from the beach was his responsibility had shaken him. Evie was older than he'd expected. Hotter than he'd expected. Wanting her made him damned uncomfortable.

Conway lifted an eyebrow. "I don't know what you mean."

"Sure you do." Jake sat in Evie's chair and glared some more. "You and Mike both gave me the impression that she was helpless, young, and in need of guidance. The woman who just left this room is none of those things. I should have gone to France," he said, disgusted.

"She's small," Conway offered with a shrug, "and looks years younger than she really is. His expression hardened and his voice turned to steel. "But the threat against her is real. Don't dismiss it. France can wait a month or two. Evie needs you." He passed a letter over. "This is a copy of what we received in the mail yesterday. Mike's mail has always been routed from the house to a box, and we pick it up. I paid all his bills, so it just made sense. But, well, read it."

Jake took the letter. Plain paper, printed out who knows where.

Evie –

Don't hit the stage. Don't sing. Don't write songs. Stay in the background where you belong, or you'll regret it.

I promise.

I never break my promises when they matter.

He resisted the urge to crush the paper in his hands. "The cops have it?" At Conway's nod, Jake scowled down at it. "This sounds like they know each other. How much does she know about the harassment?"

"A little. Not much. She thinks someone has been bothering Mike. She doesn't have a clue that it was her they were targeting. Petty stuff so far, to be sure, but Mike didn't want her to worry. For all her rough background, she's managed to retain a sweetness, almost a type of naiveté. It's damned disarming. Mike didn't want that stripped from her."

Jake met the talent manager's eyes, but didn't see any sly gleam in them. Still, he pushed. It was always good to know where people stood. "You never thought to date her?"

Surprise crossed Conway's face. "Date her? I've known her since she was fifteen. She's like a kid sister to me. I've grown very fond of her, but I wouldn't date her for the world. Plus, not my physical type."

His denial rang true, but... "What about Mike and Evie?"

Conway laughed. "They were thirty years apart, man. Mike might have been a lover in his day, but when he took Evie in, he was her protector. Nothing sexual about it for either of them. Trust me; I can sniff out forbidden relationships faster than anyone I know. They weren't lovers."

Which dovetailed with Evie's disapproval at him even asking the question. Jake frowned at the threatening note in his hand. He folded it and tucked it in the inside pocket of his suit jacket. "I'll be spending tonight at Evie's house. When I got in touch with the band earlier today, just to introduce myself, everyone said they were busy with last-minute preparations for the road trip. Tonight's her first night alone since Mike died, and I thought maybe that's not a good idea."

Conway tapped his desk. "Especially after the latest letter. How are you going to talk her into letting you stay?"

"I'll think of something. People do weird things after celebrities die, you know." What he wanted to do was take her, claim her for his own, and finish what they'd started the night before. He caught Conway's stare, and smiled coolly. "There are many different ways to get her cooperation, of course."

"Of course." Conway hesitated. "Please don't think I'm meddling, but Mike really liked you, Jake. He talked to a lot of private detectives, but he chose to trust you with the most important part of his world. He told me he didn't have a single worry about giving Evie into your care. He knew you would take care of her."

Jake grimaced. "He liked the fact that I have four sisters, but I get the feeling that's not what you're talking about. So why don't you just say plainly whatever you need to say?"

"Mike had a sense about these things." Conway tapped a pen on his desk as he thought. "Whatever happens with Evie, don't give up too soon, and don't back down. She's an amazing woman."

***

Jake drove away from the office deep in concentration as he did his best to decipher Conway's words. It was true that Mike had said to Jake's face that he was giving Evie to him. But he just thought the man had meant to watch over and care for her, and to eliminate this threat that hung over her. If he'd had the slightest inkling that he was being set up for anything else, he'd have refused outright.

But then the feel of Evie in her electric blue bikini, pressed up against him, came to mind. The kiss they shared had intoxicated him far more than the beer had. Hearing her voice today, seeing her again had been a jolt to his equilibrium. He'd been glad to take a moment in the doorway before announcing his entrance. And now he was going to spend a week on the road with her, and he was sure the big head would be arguing with the little head the entire time.

Jake hauled in a deep breath. Evie Marcherand was pure temptation. She was also, unfortunately, a client, damn it. His to care for. Younger than his youngest sister, for Pete's sake.

He'd do well to keep his hands off her.

Jake spent the rest of the drive painfully aware of an unfamiliar, wholly unwelcome, and intense excitement thrumming through his veins.

CHAPTER THREE

"Three costumes for a sixty-minute set? I know that's what Mike wanted, but don't you think that's going overboard?" They were in the living room of Mike's beach cottage, and Evie was standing on a stool. Her costumer, Joy, dark curly hair pinned up on top of her head, knelt at Evie's feet and finished basting the layered hem on the skirt of the third costume.

Joy shrugged. "Like you said, it's what Mike wanted. I'm a designer, and I do what the client wants. Within reason," she added. She got to her feet and backed up. "Okay, twirl for me."

Dutifully, Evie stepped off the stool and twirled. "You really think the dress is gonna work?" The chiffon skirt flared out, and when she stopped, it settled back down around her thighs.

"Your middle three numbers are more on the romantic side. The red one is perfect for your opener, but this dress screams romance. Look."

Evie turned to look at herself in the long mirror Joy had brought. The silk had been dyed by hand, and it looked like a wave curling to the shore—deeper blues at the top, fading in swirls to a paler blue around the asymmetrical hem. The bodice was shaped like a sundress, with a form-fitting sweetheart neckline with skinny straps and bits of silk acting like sleeves that fluttered down around her upper arms. A side zipper was her only way into and out of the dress, as it fit so well.

"It's the most beautiful thing I've ever owned. A dream of a dress. I just wish I had more up top to fill it out better." She turned and impulsively gave Joy a hug, going up on tiptoe to reach the taller woman. "Thank you so much."

Joy laughed and patted her on the back. "You are so welcome. Trust me, you don't need bigger boobs." She eased her phone out of her jeans pocket and frowned. "How can it be almost six? I'd better pack up my stuff. The hubs is due home soon." She knelt again and felt around for stray straight pins.

Evie saw the glow on her face and grinned. "Newlyweds?"

She sat back on her heels with a sigh. "Does it show? Six months. I swear, I thought I was never going to get married, but the women in my family tend not to until after they hit thirty. Not sure why," she mused. "Probably has something to do with the overprotective males in the family. May I use your bathroom?"

"Absolutely. You know the way. You've only been there twice already," she joked.

"Yeah, yeah. Now take off that dress, so I can take it with me to hem it. I'll get it to you tonight," she added as she hurried down the hall.

Evie lingered in front of the mirror. With her hair done and makeup on, she just might look like a star onstage. Which didn't help the state of her stomach one little bit.

A knock at her front door brought her out of her daydream. Opening the door and seeing Jake standing on the other side sent a sharp throb of panic through her. The tour was real. It wasn't a dream, any of it, and here was her proof, the bodyguard given to her by Mike. "What are you doing here?"

Jake didn't answer right away, and she couldn't read his eyes, hidden behind his dark shades. "You look busy." He stepped toward her, and she took a couple of steps backward, allowing him entrance.

"Panicked. Never mind. I'm just finishing up with a fitting. I need to go change, but please, have a seat. The chaise is more comfortable than it looks," she added, waving to the electric pink leather lounger. She picked up the stepstool and moved it under the coffee table.

"Evie, get that dress off. I'm running late now," Joy said as she came into the living room. Seeing Jake, she stopped in her tracks and a grin split her face. "Well hello, big brother," she said, transparently delighted, and moved in to give him a big hug. "What are you doing here? I thought you were off to France."

Jake hugged her back, rolling his eyes. He gestured toward Evie. "France got put on hold, and I'm guarding this one for a week instead. Good to see you too, oh Joyous one. Still married? I can take Thorne out, you know. All you have to do is say the word."

Joy burbled with laughter. "I am still wildly in love, but thanks for asking." She gave him a playful swat on the arm before turning to Evie. "This is one madly protective guy. You're lucky he decided to ditch France for you."

"Ooh, France. I've always wanted to go there." Evie looked from one to the other, only then seeing the resemblance in the dark hair, the set of their eyes. "Siblings, huh?"

"He's the oldest of five, the rest of us all girls. Before you say a word, Jake, I'm her costume designer. I referred your firm to Mike, but didn't realize he'd hired you." Joy reached again for Jake and gave him a smacking kiss on both cheeks. "I haven't seen you at Mom's for Sunday dinner in ages." She eyed his suit with approval. "Nice one," she said, brushing down the lapel. "But I prefer you in jeans. Oh well." She turned, made a shooing motion toward Evie. "Go. Change clothes. Hurry, woman."

Galvanized, Evie fled down the hallway to her bedroom as she wrapped her mind around the thought of Jake having sisters, barely registering Joy's footsteps behind her.

"I forgot, you'll need a little help out of this dress," Joy said as she shut the bedroom door. She turned to Evie, her face animated as she reached for the zipper. "Okay, I only have like thirty seconds, but I want you to know that Jake is the nicest guy in the world. His bark is much worse than his bite, his ex-wife is a stone bitch, and he works way too hard. He was going to France and Spain for a month to figure out his life, and he's staying here for you, so give him a break if he gets a little testy. Other than that, I think you two will really get along."

Joy's mouth ran a mile a minute as she helped Evie out of the dress and hung it on a padded hanger.

"You're a terrible matchmaker," Evie said as she dressed quickly in the tee shirt she'd worn earlier. Her mind whirled with the information given her. "Though I appreciate the fact you think I might be good enough for him."

Joy widened her eyes. "Matchmaker? Me?" She laughed and lowered her voice. "All the sisters have been trying to set him up for years. Whoever sets things in motion to get him hitched wins a free trip to Maui."

"Wow, you guys are serious."

"Once Jake is busy with his own woman and some babies, he'll leave the rest of us alone. It does make sense," she said as Evie shot her a dubious look. "And I want to win that trip. I've never been to Hawaii."

Evie giggled as she pulled on her jeans. "I stand by my earlier statement. You are a terrible matchmaker. I'm starting a career. Besides, he's years older than me. But it's sweet of you to think of it." Evie rubbed Joy's arm. She really liked the young designer and her blunt, outspoken ways.

"Give him a chance. Help him live a little." As Jake's heavier footsteps reverberated down the hall, Joy went to the door and winked. "Have some fun, that's all. You need to stretch your wings. Jake needs fun. It's a terrific match, if you ask me." She whirled around, opened the door and held the dress in front of her. "Coming through."

Evie stayed close behind, not wanting Jake in her bedroom. The last thing she needed was that visual, when she could already picture him there so clearly. She shut the door behind her, smiled briefly at Jake, and swept past him as she jogged to keep up with Joy's longer stride.

"You'll have the dress back to me tonight?"

"I promised, didn't I? Thorne and I are going to an early dinner before settling in at home. I really like the layers of skirt, and I know the shifting hemline will look gorgeous on you."

"Thank you so much. You've been great." Evie hugged her friend again and walked her outside, very aware of Jake behind her.

Joy turned halfway down the path. "Want to join Thorne and me for dinner tonight, Jake?" Her eyes twinkled.

Evie watched closely, but Jake merely smiled. "Have fun, kiddo. Love you."

Joy grinned. "Love you, too. Bye. Be good, you two. But not too good," and she waggled her eyebrows. "If you know what I mean."

Evie could feel her cheeks heat up at the innuendo. She waited until Joy drove off before turning to the doorway where Jake lounged, looking irritatingly like he belonged there. She raised her brows. "To what do I owe the honor? We don't leave until tomorrow."

"I understand the band has abandoned you," he said. "Thought I'd bunk here tonight, since I know there's room." He backed away from the door and gestured her in. "This place has, what, three bedrooms?"

"Four, but one is a music room." She frowned as she followed. "Is there a reason I shouldn't be alone? I'm surrounded by neighbors I've known for years, you know." She watched as he wandered, checking on windows, peeking into the kitchen.

"Apparently there was a news item. Mike's death, you now own the house he lived in, that kind of thing. I don't want you here alone, great neighbors or not. It'll all die down, eventually." He said it as if it were something to be expected. "Or you can take Joy's word for it, and say it's just my protective streak coming through. I'm going to check the rest of the house. Be right back." He disappeared down the hallway.

Evie nibbled on her thumb. She'd read enough about celebrities and people taking advantage of the loved ones left behind. She'd never expected to be one of those people that others would bother with. Funny.

Jake came back into the living room. "I put the safety on all the windows and locked the deadbolt on the back door. I also turned on the outdoor security lights. You're not used to keeping everything locked up, are you?"

"No. I hadn't thought." She gazed around the room, gave a soft sigh. "I guess I'll have to sell this place at some point." The thought hurt. She loved it. Every room screamed *Mike* to her, from the pink leather chaise, the orange club chairs, and the jam-packed bookshelves, to the wooden floors and bright Mexican rag rugs scattered about. It wasn't exactly her taste, but it had been so right for Mike.

"Mike gave you to me to protect and care for. I will do everything in my power to keep you safe." The emotion in his voice seemed to surprise him, for he took a swift breath. "Damned protective streak. I'm sure Joy filled you in." He rubbed the back of his neck.

Searching his face, his eyes, she could see he meant every word underneath his embarrassment. Warmth unfurled in her belly. "You know, last night. On the beach. I haven't kissed anyone in a very long time."

"You haven't forgotten how," he quipped. "You all packed? It's only for a week, but we go to meet the bus early tomorrow. Best to get all your packing done tonight."

She took a breath to steady herself. So he didn't want to talk about it. Fine. "Yes, all done. There isn't much I'll need. What about you? Are you all packed?"

"Done and done. Put it on the bus, except for an overnight bag. So, what should we do now?"

"Since you don't want to talk about the amazing chemistry we have, how do pizza and a movie sound? Ciro's delivers," she added. "Or, now that I think about it, do guard dogs only eat raw meat?"

"Not funny," he said, but smiled, once again ignoring her reference to the night before. "And as Ciro's is my favorite, make it a large with everything. I'll be right back. I want to do a check on the perimeter."

Evie ordered the pizza and looked through Mike's extensive collection of movies, trying not to think of this as a date. Especially since he'd decided that the kiss had never happened. She had to admit to disappointment, but perhaps it was understandable. They were going to be working together. If they got too personal, it might make things sticky.

His spending the night was part of the job, that's all. Jake was her friend and bodyguard.

She stilled, one hand clutching the first *Lord of the Rings* movie, while the other had a grip on the *Three Stooges*. Her *friend?* She'd known him less than a day. She'd shared a kiss with him even before she knew his name. Now he was her bodyguard, bought and paid for by Mike. How did any of that equal "friend"?

***

After a *Three Stooges* movie and a couple pieces of pizza, plus a last-minute visit from Joy with the finished costume, Evie said goodnight and headed to bed, where she fell asleep almost instantly. A noise, something in the night, woke her a couple hours later, and for a moment she thought to check on Mike. She remembered before her feet hit the floor and scrambled back under the sheet. It had only been a month, and some habits were hard to break.

The house was dark, silent. She bunched the pillow beneath her head and stared up at the ceiling. Mike was gone, but he'd given her Jake.

Jake seemed, well, nice. Slightly dangerous. He was even a bit of a stuffed shirt, except when it came to kissing. Then add in his love for the Stooges…Evie sighed. Not that any of that added up to a single male type. She'd never met anyone quite like Jake.

Were all men just little boys at heart? It seemed like it. Get the band together and you could count on fart jokes and snickers anytime someone said the number sixty-nine.

Brad Gaines hadn't ever been a little boy, though.

Damn it. Evie squinched her eyes shut.

Brad, her childhood hero, had been hovering at the back of her thoughts since Mike's death. She shifted and tried to bring his face to her mind. But all that came to her was thick, brown, curling hair that drooped slightly over one brown eye, chiseled cheeks, and a tan that came from an expensive salon. Merely images from his photos in the entertainment magazines she'd seen a bit ago. That was all she had.

She couldn't see any resemblance to the scruffy kid who'd rescued her when she was six and he was eight, nor the young man who'd taken her virginity, willingly given, the spring she'd turned fifteen.

She couldn't even clearly see the seventeen-year-old kid who'd run out on her that summer, taking her trust, her love, everything that mattered. For pity's sakes, why had she even thought of him? Why now, after all these years?

Restless, she got up and padded into the kitchen for a glass of water. Brad had his own career and had done well for himself. She stopped following him years ago. It hurt too much, especially when his first big hit had sounded too much like a song they had worked on together. They were supposed to hit the big time together, damn it.

Evie blew out a breath, telling herself to let the resentment go. Mike had given her so much, and part of what he'd given her had been the time to grow up in safety. Now her career was finally starting, and she needed to leave the past alone. What was done could not be undone. Shakespeare said it, so it must be true.

If only she still had her first notebook, the one where she'd poured out years of lyrics and songs and emotions, the one thing she had clung to, that had held her identity. Losing it, then losing Brad a week or so later, had just about gutted her. She'd never taken the time to recreate any of those songs, those lyrics. For years it had been too painful. Maybe now, during downtime on the bus, she would be able to get a start on it. Maybe. Things had changed, and she'd written new songs since then, but still.

She finished off the glass of water. It cooled her throat, easing the unshed tears gathered there. She put the glass down, looked to the hallway leading to the bedrooms, and wondered.

***

Jake woke from a sound sleep to see the door to the bedroom ease open, a paler gray rectangle against the darkness of that corner of the room. He rose up on his elbow, alert. "Evie? Is that you?"

A soft sigh came from the doorway. "Sorry. Habit. I think I hear something and the next thing I know, I'm checking on Mike."

The summer night was still warm, despite their proximity to the beach. The ceiling fan turned lazy circles, mingling their scents with the jasmine that bloomed outside. Moonlight filtered in through the wide window and crickets chirped in a random pattern.

Jake allowed himself to relax.

He sat up and leaned against the padded headboard, making sure the sheet covered him up to his waist. "You want to talk?"

"Do you mind?" She came in, leaving the door ajar, and settled on the foot of the bed. Her sleep outfit consisted of silk boxer shorts and a tank top, both in a sunny yellow. "This is when I miss him the most. This time of night. The last couple of weeks I would sing him back to sleep if he woke. He needed the company."

Sympathy softened his voice. "I'm sorry. He seemed like a really cool guy." Jake did his best to look anywhere except where her firm breasts pushed against the silk. They would fit perfectly in his hands…wrong thought. He cleared his throat and tried not to breathe in her scent.

"Mmm. He was a cool guy. Cool, but stupid, too. I mean, almost no one dies of AIDS anymore. Not in this country, anyway."

He was not in the mood for sadness. He didn't think she really was, either. "Mike told me about that. Said he was more afraid of doctors and their cures than dying. He cracked me up with all his talk. But you know what I did after our first conversation?"

"Called your doctor?"

He chuckled, relieved at her smile. "Yeah. Got my first checkup in years. Healthy, which I figured I was since I'm pretty careful."

She settled in, wiggling around to get comfortable. "Tell me about yourself. You know about me. All I know about you is that you have sisters, and one of them is a talented designer named Joy."

He didn't see the harm in talking. At least it kept his mind off kissing her. He rubbed his left forearm and thought about his family. "All of us were born here in San Diego. My mom stayed home to raise us kids, while my father was a trucker. Our life went to hell the day he died in a big rig accident, up near Los Angeles. Tied up the freeway for hours and our lives for years."

She reached out and squeezed his foot. "I'm so sorry."

He pulled up his knees, moving out of her reach. Her touching him right now, in the deep of the night, was too much of a temptation. He focused on his story instead of his rising need for her. "I was nineteen, working and going to college. My dad's death changed everything. I moved back home. Worked, transferred to UCSD, lived close to Mom. Got married and divorced."

"You keep rubbing your arm. What is it?" She shifted toward him to see.

He leaned forward and stuck out his left arm, not wanting her too close. "After I left Berkeley but before I got home, I got this tattoo."

She traced a finger down the names. "Jennifer, Janelle, Jacey, and Joy. What's next to their names? A heart?" She looked up, and her lips were just inches away from his. "That's so sweet."

He pulled away from her and wrapped his arms around his knees again. Enough was enough, and he'd just hit his limit. "Yeah. Stupid. Hey, you should get back to bed. It's going to be a long day, and it's already after two in the morning."

Evie sat back, crossed her arms. "I know you like wearing suits, but I didn't think someone who could kiss the way you do could be so damned stuffy." Amusement warred with irritation in her voice.

"I'm not stuffy." God, he *sounded* stuffy.

"You are. You're nervous, too. Why?"

His overriding concern spilled out. "Because I got married just a few weeks after my dad died. I know how grief can alter a young person's reality, how something you'd never normally do suddenly seems the height of rationality. I want to spare you those mistakes." Jake's heart thumped hard, the sound loud in is ears.

Evie ducked her head so he couldn't see her face. For a long minute, she didn't say a word. She took a breath, blew it out. Shook her head.

"Wow. You want to spare me. From what? Ravishing you? Proposing? Planning a wedding?" She shoved off the bed and went to the door. There she hesitated and turned just a little back toward him. "If you're not careful, they'll be asking you for your AARP card at the movies soon. And for the record? If you were trying to talk me out of having sex with you, you've succeeded." The door closed behind her with a decided *snick* of temper.

Good. She was gone.

Damn it. Jake jumped out of the bed, cursing under his breath. He rummaged for a pair of jeans and tugged them on over his hardening cock, doing up most of the buttons on the fly but not bothering with a shirt. She was the most frustrating, sexy, infuriating, sexy, confusing woman he'd ever met. He flung his door open and, seeing light from down the hallway, headed to the kitchen where she had pulled the leftover pizza out of the fridge and set it on the island countertop.

He stopped, keeping the island between them, his temper sizzling. "I wasn't trying to talk you out of having sex. We haven't even gotten to the part where we can talk each other *into* having sex. I am dead serious. I know what it's like to have the stable force in your life suddenly disappear. I know how rocked your world is right now. I don't want to add to that."

She gripped the edge of the counter. Emotion swirled in her dark eyes. "Tell me this. Did you know who I was on the beach last night?"

"What? No. Of course not." Offended, he slapped the counter. "Do you think I was spying on you?"

She cut him off with a gesture. "Just wait. Why didn't you follow me? I invited you. I could have sworn I was going to see you very soon, walking up to the bonfire, looking for me. Why didn't you show? If you had, we'd have already had sex and gotten it over with."

His desire and his temper flared. "Not that I have to explain, but okay. First off, I don't do one-night stands. Second, I was starting a new job the next day. I didn't know how long I'd be gone, or how long the job would last. That is no way to start a relationship, so I relegated you to a fantasy and let it go. Third, us already having had sex would not have made tonight any easier. I don't know where you got that idea."

Her eyes widened. "You labeled me a fantasy?"

Heat burned through him. "Did we share that amazing kiss under the moonlight? That was you in the electric blue bikini, right?" He watched as she swallowed hard. God, he wanted her.

Her breath came a little faster. "Yes. That was me."

"Okay then. Okay." He took a breath and wiped his face with one hand. He needed to dial it back or he'd be stripping her, bending her over the island. Plunging into her body. Damn it, he chastised himself silently, don't go there. "Give me a piece of pizza, and no one gets hurt."

The heat in her eyes eased into humor. "That's it? I think I'm still pissed off," she said, handing him a piece of pizza. "Do you want a plate or a paper towel?"

"Paper towel." He took a bite of pizza and let out a little groan. "Still good." Not as good as sex, but that rather went without saying. Too bad his cock was still on the whole "let's have sex now" trip. At least the island hid the obvious.

He caught the crumpled paper towel she sent flying toward him and watched as she sat at one of the barstools at the counter and picked up the second-to-last slice.

She lifted her chin and set it in what he was beginning to recognize as her stubborn look. "So, what are we going to do about this thing between us?"

"Want milk?" At her nod, Jake put his pizza down and went to the fridge. Poured the last of the carton into one glass. "We'll have to share. No milk for cereal tomorrow, either."

She grinned suddenly, catching him off guard. "That must be from taking care of your sisters. Men don't usually think about milk for breakfast when they're eating pizza after two-something in the morning."

"I don't know about that. I used to eat cereal for dinner at times. I have always watched the milk consumption, wherever I lived." He eyed her in some confusion. "You're not mad anymore. Why?"

She shrugged. "Mike knew what he was doing, sending you to me. I trusted him with my life, so I trust you. Plus, we shared an amazing kiss. And you thought of bikini-me as a fantasy, which makes it kind of hard to stay mad." She flashed him another grin. "I mean, seriously. I've never been anyone's fantasy before."

"Never? I doubt that."

Her smile faded, a shadow crossed her face as she finished off her pizza. "One piece left. I've got yogurt in the fridge for breakfast tomorrow, so I'll leave this last piece for you. Assuming you do the man thing of pizza for breakfast," she added. "Nice way to duck my question, by the way."

He hadn't ducked it. He'd purposely ignored it. The slice sat in his stomach like a lump. "What do we do about this thing between us? You're my client, Evie. You're grieving."

"None of that mattered on the beach last night. That kiss was, well. I'll never forget it." Her gaze, intent on him, made him want to squirm.

"You're younger than my youngest sister. I'm too old for you. There are fourteen years between us," he began, only to be interrupted by her strangled shriek.

She picked up the empty pizza box and thumped herself on the forehead with it. "I *knew* you were fixated on the age thing. I don't *care*. It doesn't *matter*. Age is nothing compared to attitude. Age I can handle, but not a *stuffy attitude*."

"Stuffy attitude? You don't know what you're talking about."

"Great. Now I'm stupid, to boot." She tossed the box onto the counter, blew out a breath and stood. "That's it. I'm going to bed. Alone, apparently. You know the only good thing about this argument? You're in here, shirtless, sockless, and wearing very tight jeans that show just how *uninterested* in me you are. All of which mitigates your stuffiness. Just a little."

She went to sweep past him, her chin in the air, but he stepped in her way, reached out, and swept her up. "You want sex? I'll give you sex." He covered her mouth with his and pressed her close, lifting her off her feet and holding her against him. He groaned as her hands urged him closer, caressing the bare skin of his back before locking around his neck.

Jake swore he could hear the sound of the waves cresting on the shore. The silk of her shirt melted into the silk of her skin so Jake could barely tell where one ended and the other began. Her scent made him lightheaded, a little bit crazy as he kissed her, driven by need and desperation.

Her taste, the feel of her against him, sank deep into his very bones and he knew he'd never get her out of his system if he didn't stop holding her, kissing her. He eased his lips from hers, pressed kisses down her throat, stopping at her collarbone. That was his "Do Not Cross" line that he'd dreamed up, years ago, and stayed above unless he was prepared to go all the way. He wasn't. He hadn't packed any condoms on purpose.

He dragged in a breath and set her away from him. "I couldn't let you go to sleep without a goodnight kiss."

She took a step to him, reached up and touched his lips before trailing her fingers down his throat and across his chest. She smiled—a siren's smile. "I never would have guessed you had hair on your chest." She combed her fingers through it.

Jake's nipples tightened and he sucked in another breath, again stepping just out of her reach. "I'm not into manscaping. Disappointed?"

She eyed him.

Jake repressed a groan as her visual survey turned his body rigid, his cock pressed painfully against the buttons of his jeans. He watched as she licked her lips before dragging her gaze back up to his face.

"Nope. But I sure hope you let go of your stuffy misconceptions soon."

He rolled his eyes. "Go to bed."

She winked at him. "Lock your door." She headed down the hallway, her hips swaying in a sassy manner. He watched until she disappeared into her bedroom.

Jake put the extra slice of pizza back in the box and stuck it in the nearly empty fridge. He tossed the paper towels, and downed the milk they'd both forgotten to drink. He rinsed the glass, put it on the dish drainer, and flipped out the light.

He thought she might be joking about locking his door. But after brushing his teeth and settling himself to sleep, he had second thoughts. Getting out of bed, he padded naked over to the door to lock it.

If there was one thing Jake had learned to be good at, it was delaying gratification.

CHAPTER FOUR

Evie bent her head to the guitar. *"Life on the streets/well it ain't so pretty/dodging the beats/fighting the johns/so I made my way/to Ocean City/the sand was so warm and/the waves were a song."* Evie shook her head, made a notation on the pad in front of her and stretched her fingers. Looked around at the rear lounge in appreciation.

When they'd first boarded, she'd made a beeline for one of the bunks in the center of the large bus. After that middle-of-the-night encounter with Jake, she'd stayed awake for hours, melodies and lyrics chasing themselves round and round in her mind even while she replayed spreading her hand across the heavy muscles of his chest. By the time the bus had actually gotten on the road, she'd been sound asleep.

A brief stop for lunch had her waking up. She had been surprised to see the band there with them, but took the explanation of their bus breaking down in stride. There was plenty of room for three more people.

It also had the added appeal of three more people to keep Jake distracted. He'd been on his computer in the front lounge since lunchtime, so she'd come to the rear lounge to sing and write, tucking herself into a corner of the U-shaped, deep-cushioned seating.

Evie sighed and went back to her song, one of the ones she'd be debuting on this tour. *"That's when I met/the Soul Savior/the beach was his pulpit /the sermon his song/he took me in/taught me forgiveness/I let down my guard and/ I let him be strong.*

A knocking on the open entryway made her grin. "Come in."

Jake sauntered in, looking sexier than ever in jeans, a tee shirt, and a plaid shirt over that. "Sounding good. Just checking in on you. Everything okay?"

"Yeah." She shrugged. "Working on one of the songs I'll be singing. Playing with some new words."

"Mining your past, I see." He sat on one long side of the U, his body angled toward her.

Insulted and not willing to admit it, she stared at him. "For someone who has never heard my songs, that sounded remarkably like a dig." She raised her eyebrows. "Is that a dig?"

"Hell no," he said, surprised. "But I thought you'd made the trek from El Cajon to the beach what, over ten years ago? Surely there's got to be something more interesting to write about now."

"This is Mike's song. I wrote it for him last year. He hated being called a soul savior, blustered about it a lot. But I'd catch him humming the tune and grinning to himself, so I'm pretty sure he liked it." Evie took a breath and called on all her powers of patience. "Anyway. No one knows me as a songwriter. Not yet. Most of what I've written since Mike took me under his wing has never seen the light of day, or been played in concert. This will be only the second time I've sung some of these songs in front of an audience. I didn't even sing at his wake."

His eyes cooled as he seemed to digest her explanation. "So, you can't rush the creative spirit? Need to hang out in the old neighborhood, I suppose. The songs make you sound sad. I guess that's what digs at me." He stood, caught the edge of the doorway as the bus swayed.

"Anyway, we're due in to the hotel in a couple of hours. You and I have a date at the club tonight, to check it out and see the act, hear the acoustics, et cetera. There even might be a spotlight on you, saying hey, she's here tomorrow night."

"I know, I know, I've got the itinerary." She rolled her eyes and he chuckled.

"I'm going. Keep on, you know…being creative, or whatever." He disappeared down the hallway to the front lounge.

Evie frowned at his retreating back. Was she repeating herself? She ran down her list of songs. "Last Girl Down," "Soul Savior," "Run Hell for Leather," "You Stole Me," "Hang On for Dear Life." And that was just a fraction of the songs she'd written.

Restless, she set her guitar back in its case, put her notebook inside and closed it up before she went out to talk to the others.

Jimmy and Reid were asleep in the bunks. Rhoads, driving, had his wife to chat with. Jake had both earplugs tapped into his laptop and didn't bother to look up when she passed. Only Bear sat alone, just kind of staring into space.

Evie went to sit next to the big drummer. His nickname was in relation to his size; at six foot two inches and at least two-eighty, Bear was a big man who knew how to handle the drums. He was also one of Evie's favorites.

Bear picked up her hand in one of his. "How ya doin', sweetheart?"

She leaned her head on his beefy shoulder and sighed. "I'm okay."

"Nuh-unh. Don't believe you. Is it Mike?"

Wistfulness slid through her at his question. "No. I mean, yes, it will always hit me that he's gone, but this is different. Can I ask you a question?"

He rumbled out a laugh. "Sure. Got nothing else to do."

She gnawed on her thumbnail. "I don't know how to ask this, so I'll just ask. Is my music too, I don't know. Last decade?"

Bear swung his big head around to look at her. His long, bushy beard brushed her forehead and she sat up with a grin. Bear searched her eyes. "Do you mean, does it sound old?"

"No. But is it, could it be, too young for me?" She worried her left thumbnail with her teeth.

"Well now, that depends. Have you outgrown singing those songs?"

"I don't know." Evie tugged at the fingernail. Jake had confused her. Damn it. "They seem better suited for a younger girl at this point. You know. A teenager."

Bear gently pushed her finger out of her mouth. "Don't bite your nails," he chided. "As far as your music goes, it depends on you, sweetheart. You never have to relive those days unless you want to. You've just been growin' up, and you probably have a lot of new songs inside you. That's just fine. Let 'em out. See how they fly."

"It's not like we can try something new during this tour." She pressed a hand against her belly at the thought of playing for a paying audience. "If I have the strength to do the ones we've got," she added.

Bear laughed. "If you've got something new to share, we'll all take a look at it. We love you. Working with you is like honoring Mike, you know? And we loved him a lot. Owe him a lot."

"I know. And you're sweet." She reached up and kissed his bushy cheek. She loved the band like family, and they'd known each other for a long time now.

Bear cleared his throat. "There's one thing to consider, about your songs. You're not like that pretty young thing, that Taylor Swift. You don't talk about high school, and you don't talk about first love, and your melodies aren't all light and fluffy. You're about hardship, and fighting for safety, and finding home. Your words are raw, and you wear your bloodied heart on your sleeve. There's nothing 'specially young about either of those things."

Evie sat back, her eyes widening as she absorbed what he was saying. "You're right."

He patted her hand. "Now, that don't mean there aren't other topics, or that other songs may be coming out of you that are nothin' like what's gone in the past. And that's okay, too. That's great. Because every artist needs to grow. That Taylor, she don't sing about high school n'more." Bear yawned a big one. "I'm gonna get some shut eye, sweetheart. Stayed up too late last night."

To her amusement, Bear closed his eyes and fell into a light, even sleep. She squeezed his arm and stared out the window opposite.

Every artist needs to grow.

What, exactly, does an artist need to grow her craft? She was practically weaned on disappointment and heartbreak. If she looked to the past couple of years, it was still heartbreak, but of a different kind. Watching Mike die a slow death was one of the hardest things she'd ever done.

But there was joy, too, her heart whispered. And what about all those strange, new feelings Jake brought into her life? Two days ago, she wouldn't have even considered her songs as being a part of her past. But maybe he was right. She wasn't that skinny teen who ran away from a scary living situation. Not anymore.

That boy, the one who had stolen her heart and so much more when he'd left almost eleven long years ago, was barely on her mental horizon now. She had freedom, she had this opportunity in front of her, she had talent, and she had friends.

The only person who could screw it up was herself. She had too much pride to let everything she'd worked for fall apart.

She stood and made her way back to the lounge at the back of the bus. Jake was there, stretched out on one of the padded couches, his arm over his eyes. While she'd been thinking, he'd left and she'd hardly even noticed.

Evie sat opposite him and opened her guitar case, settled the instrument on her knee, and allowed herself the luxury of staring at him. She fingerpicked notes quietly.

What did she know about him? Other than he had four sisters and an abundance of the protective gene. Other than he could kiss her senseless. She knew the hair on his chest was crisp yet soft against her hand. That his skin reacted to her touch. That he liked her favorite type of pizza and preferred to drink milk with it.

She knew his scent. It drew her in, made her want. She felt safe with him around. She frowned. Why safe? Was it because Mike had decreed it so, without telling her, without allowing her to argue with him?

Both she and Mike had tempers. They'd had their fights, Lord knew. Both of them, luckily, tended to get over being angry easily. Would Mike have laughed at her concerns about growing close to Jake so quickly, or encouraged her to take him and the feelings she had for him with a barrel of doubt?

The melody she played turned wistful as she watched him sleep. Part of her wished they'd already had sex so she could curl up next to him, and that she had the right to do so. What she would give to run her hands through his dark hair, touch the planes of his face, his strong nose. To press kisses on him that he would return, his face filled with passion, or laughter. Evie played, and daydreamed, and filled herself with the sight of the man opposite her.

He chose that moment to move his arm and look at her. Raw emotion shone in those eyes for a brief, unguarded second, and she caught her breath. Her fingers stilled on the strings.

His lids shielded his gaze. "I liked that song. What was it?"

She blinked, looked down at her fingers. "I don't know. I was noodling. No words, yet."

"So it's a wisp of a thread of a song?" He turned toward her, rose up on his elbow and propped his head up with his hand. "I like it a lot."

She flushed and busied herself with wiping down the strings with part of an old flannel shirt. "Thanks."

"You're talented. I'm going to enjoy following your career."

"You don't have to say that. God. You're like, my babysitter. Bequeathed to me by my deceased—what. He wasn't my dad. Friend. Okay. Employer, since he paid me. Taught me what a checking account was, and how to use it. Made sure I put money into savings each month and didn't spend everything. Got me through school. He—oh man." Evie put both hands across her mouth as her cheeks burned in embarrassment. "Sorry," she mumbled.

"I guess you needed to get that out." Jake sat up, brushed the hair out of his eyes. "But he was more than that. He was a mentor to you. Did you have any other mentors? Anyone else you trusted?"

"Not like Mike." Weak tears, the ones she hadn't shed when he died, welled up. "He taught me everything. I don't know who I'd be right now if not for him." She blinked, willing the tears away.

Jake nodded. "I get that. He was a fixer. He needed to fix people, or at the least, help them along their way. So you've never known anyone like that before?"

"A fixer? Yeah, that fits. No. He's the first. He's done it with every band member, though. Whatever they needed, he saw they got." She tilted her head and considered him. "How do you know that?"

He laughed a little, scrubbed his face before dropping his hands. "He'd done his homework. Not only did he find, and support, my sister Joy in her costuming endeavor, not to mention her *haute couture* designing, but once he found her, he found my other sister, Janelle, who runs the High Tea Palace in San Carlos. His largesse extends out from there. As you heard, Joy put him in touch with me."

She strummed an E chord. "How did you get in the bodyguard business?"

He laughed again, rubbed his neck. "When my dad died, I became responsible for my sisters and my mom."

"Hence their names on your forearm," she added.

"Yes. So. They would get asked out on dates. Of course, being the man of the family, I needed to clear these punks before I could let them go out."

"Oh no, you didn't." Evie knew her eyes were wide even as she stifled a giggle.

He arched his eyebrows. "Oh yes I did. Then things around the neighborhood started happening. Break-ins, stupid ones. Small acts of vandalism. So I started a neighborhood watch group in the area. Just the local teens being stupid, but having the neighborhood involved soon put a stop to the petty crime."

She could totally see it. "So what did you do then?"

"I changed my major to law enforcement. Eventually joined the San Diego Police Force. Had expected to retire with them, but left after five years."

Evie sat back, impressed. "Why'd you leave? I mean, five years. It's hard to get onto the force to begin with, isn't it?"

He shrugged. "It ended up not being a good fit for me. Going private seemed to work better for a long time. Then, of course, I decided to do some travel."

"Ah, that's right. The delayed vacation. Why France and Spain?"

"Thinking of changing careers. France seemed to be a good place to do some serious thinking, and I've always wanted to see Spain."

Rhoads came over the loudspeaker. "We're pulling in to Vegas, folks. ETA to the hotel, fifteen minutes."

Evie and Jake shared a look. She grinned, a sense of adventure bubbling up inside her. "I've never been out of California."

He stretched his arms over his head and grinned back at her. "You're in Nevada now. Come on, let's go up front and see Las Vegas."

***

Hours later, Jake watched as Evie checked out the room where she'd be performing, a small club inside their hotel at the far northern end of the strip. The afternoon had been fun if exhausting as she'd dragged him from one end of the town to the other in her excitement to see everything, as bouncy as a little kid. Now, she looked all business. A new side of her that he hadn't seen before. He had to admit, her business persona was sexy as hell.

The club was between sets, and Evie talked closely with the club manager, a big walrus of a guy with a mustache to match and blinding-white teeth that weren't his own. Jake didn't trust him at first sight, but then that had been the case with everyone Evie had talked to that day. He didn't trust any of them. Anyone she'd flashed her bright smile to had come under his intense scrutiny.

He'd been lucky to intercept a threatening message for her at the hotel. It was luckier still that he'd been able to talk to the hotel manager. No more messages were to go to Evie directly but were to be sent to him.

She didn't need to know someone was very unhappy about her fledgling career. He'd just wished she'd talked to him when he gave her the opening, earlier on the bus. He knew she'd had another music mentor. Mike had kind of mentioned it but had been sketchy on the details, because that was the one part of her past Evie had refused to talk about.

Jake shared Mike's gut feeling that this unknown guy was the key.

Jake narrowed his eyes at her across the club. He needed Evie to tell him everything. But how could he get her to spill her secrets, when she hadn't even told the man she trusted the most?

Her laugh came to him then, low and throaty. Walrus Man patted her on the ass and Jake took a deep breath even as red hazed his vision. Evie shifted and grabbed both his hands in hers, her tone a laughing put-down. Jake relaxed as he saw her handle Grabby Hands. He stayed where he was, propping up the back wall of the club, and imagined taking the big man down.

His protective instincts were on target. He thought they might get rusty, as Joy had married six months previously, but his reaction to Evie proved they were as strong as ever. Though he had to admit he couldn't quite get a handle on thinking of Evie as his sister. When his sisters had worn skin-tight miniskirts, he'd wanted to cover them with a blanket. He didn't have that reaction when he'd first seen Evie tonight. On the contrary.

Her heart-stopping red dress fit her like a glove and, as far as he could guess, she wasn't wearing a stitch underneath it. It made his hands itch to touch the silky skin. No, a blanket wasn't what he had in mind. Instead, he'd start at her three-inch, black patent leather heels and slide his hands up her legs, worshipping them. Tickle the back of her knees until she laughed, then lick there until she moaned. Continue his way up her legs until he could slide the dress up, baring her body to his gaze.

Baring her sex to his lips. He'd—someone thumped him on the arm. He blinked and looked around.

"Jake." Evie thumped him again, her eyes filled with laughter. "Wow, were you gone. That must have been some daydream."

He grinned. "You have no idea. Are you done here? Did you want to stay?"

She looked around the place wistfully. "I do, but I'm tired. Didn't get much sleep last night."

"Then let's go upstairs. Do you have a routine before shows?" He placed his hand low on her back as they walked out the club. The cheerful jangle of the slot machines assaulted them, and Jake winced, bending down to hear her better. "You know, three hours of sleep, a big plate of pasta four hours before show time, a spritz of your favorite perfume, that kind of thing."

"No routine. Haven't done enough shows to have a routine," she said, pitching her voice louder so she could be heard. "I guess I'm not important enough."

Jake, bent toward her, turned to look at her even as she looked up at him. Their lips were a whisper apart, and they stopped right where they were, caught by possibility.

"Hey, watch it, lovebirds," snapped a waitress. "Walking here." She detoured around them with a full tray of drinks and headed toward the slot machines.

They both took a breath and looked forward as they continued to the elevators.

CHAPTER FIVE

Need tightened Jake's every muscle. They waited, silent, for the elevator. He desperately wanted to know what she was thinking but had nothing to say to her that wouldn't sound like a come-on. Tomorrow was a big night for her. He didn't want to do anything to screw that up, so he'd just better hang on to his control and take a damned cold shower.

Or two.

Whatever would get him through the night.

The elevator finally arrived and he ushered her in. He hit the button for their floor and leaned back against the mirrored wall, gripping the bar that ran around the inside edge of the elevator, and made the mistake of taking a deep breath.

She'd worn a different perfume tonight, something exotic that went along with the makeup she'd used to great effect. She looked less like a beach girl and much more like a wanton siren, luring men and ships to a rocky death.

Jake tightened his grip as Evie sidled closer to him.

"What's wrong?" Her smoky-sweet voice sliced through his pretense.

"Nothing." The heat from her body tempted. The daydream he'd had in the club didn't help. Her closeness, that dress, the perfume all pulled at his resolve to keep his hands off her.

She leaned back against the bar, her hip resting next to his hand. If he turned his palm up, he'd be able to cup her ass. He gave a silent thanks as the elevator slid to a stop and the doors opened.

But Evie didn't move, so he pinched her behind and she jumped ahead with a little squeal. She turned to shoot him a dirty look, but he just hustled her out of the elevator to where he could breathe a little easier.

That lasted until they stopped in front of her room. "Will you come in?" Evie had opened the door and now stood, holding it wide for him. "Please?"

"Evie." Oh God. Why did turning her down feel so wrong? "Your first big show is tomorrow night. Nothing else between us has changed. You should get some sleep."

48

He expected something dramatic from her. Tears, maybe. Scorn. A tantrum. Something.

Instead, she just looked at him steadily, the door open, leaving the decision up to him. No demands made, other than her need, so clear on her face.

It killed him. She looked so vulnerable. His heart in his throat, he moved in, kissed her on the cheek and took the doorknob in his hand. "I'm right on the other side of the connecting door if you need me for anything. Sleep well. I'll join you for breakfast in the morning, okay?" With a step backward, he pulled the door shut between them. "Throw the privacy lock on, Evie. Please." He waited until he heard the lock click home before moving into his own room, feeling as though he had just missed out on the biggest adventure of his life.

***

Evie stared at the ceiling of her hotel room. Close to three in the morning, and she couldn't get to sleep to save her life. Nerves like she'd never had before had her stomach upset.

She'd so been hoping she and Jake could do the mattress mambo. She had the sneaking suspicion a full dose of Jake would definitely help her relax, if not put her into a sated stupor. But it was not to be. So instead, she'd done a full yoga workout and drank the chamomile tea that came with the room. Both teabags. She read until her eyes were blurry. She'd finally resorted to taking a hot bath.

Nothing. Even counting the faint gold swirls on the ceiling hadn't worked. Disgusted with herself, she pushed the covers off, flipped on a bedside light and went to rescue her guitar from its case. That new melody, the one she'd been doodling while daydreaming about Jake, wouldn't leave her alone. Which meant it was time to think about lyrics.

Settled on the couch, she checked the sound. Sure enough, it was still in tune from her playing earlier. She picked softly at the strings, finding her way back to the melody that had been haunting her since that afternoon.

Words for it remained elusive. She played what she thought of as the verse then segued into the chorus. Slightly melancholy, a bit wistful, yet the chorus had a lilting melody that, depending on the words, could be uplifting. Hopeful.

It all came down to using the right words.

Brad had never said the right words.

At the thought, she stopped playing in surprise. Why had it taken her so long to see that? At fifteen, she'd still been so young, so when he'd said they'd stick together, she'd actually thought he'd meant it. Even when he was making plans to take their music on the road, he'd kept saying they'd stick together, without ever being clear as to what her role would be.

It had taken him leaving her in the dead of night, sneaking out of the house with his older brother, for her to finally realize that he hadn't meant "him and her" when he'd said "they." Blood, she'd reflected bitterly, had been thicker than the love he'd professed for her.

She bit her thumbnail to the quick, hissed at the sting of pain. Began to play again.

Jake, on the other hand, was a man who knew the power of words. The only thing that kept her from dragging him into her room had been his obvious concern about her first club performance. He'd said the right words, and he'd meant them.

Brad had never said the right words. Or he'd never meant them. But why was he metaphorically slapping her in the face now? She hadn't thought of him this much in years.

A knock came on the connecting door. Jake. She set aside the guitar and flew to the door, expectation making her tremble. She unlocked it to find him, shirtless and wearing jeans, sitting cross-legged on the other side. His door had been propped wide open, and the room behind him was dark.

"I like the new song." He glanced up at her. "Even though you don't have lyrics yet."

Simple. Powerful. Yes, he knew his way around words. Evie cleared her throat and sat facing him, her back against the doorjamb. "You couldn't sleep either, huh?"

"Nope." His hair flopped down into his eyes and he brushed it back. "I'm guessing I'll be taking a long afternoon nap. This hanging around with celebrities is rough."

"Yeah, right. Celebrities." She wrapped her arms around her knees and leaned her head back. "I miss the ocean. I mean, the desert is nice, but I miss the ocean, and we've been gone, what. Not even a whole day. The air here is hard. You know?"

"I know what you mean. I miss it, too, even though I don't live as close to it as you do."

"Where do you live?"

He shifted closer to her side, took her hand in his. "Near Balboa Park. I ride my bike through the park, or I jog. It's not the beach, but it is beautiful."

She stared down at the tattoo of his sisters' names on his forearm. She twisted her hand free of his and ran a finger over the names and the symbols next to them. "What do these mean? The hearts? And this one, crossed out?"

He took her hand again, his thumb making lazy circles on her skin. "I get the hearts after each sister gets married. With Jennifer, the oldest girl, she married someone I didn't trust, but six months in they were still married, and she still professed her love for him. So I got a heart. She divorced him a year later, hence the crossed out heart."

What a softie. She pointed to the last name on his arm. "Joy is married, and she doesn't have a heart after her name. Why?"

"It hasn't been a year yet. Thorne is a great guy, and I fully expect them to make it, but I'm still watching over them until the marriage is a year old." He shrugged. "It's a hard habit to break."

She raised her eyebrows. "I'd think their men would hate you for it."

"Yeah, well, they're just like me. So they understand. They don't like it, but they get it."

That macho, take-care-of-women thing. Huh. "You're not the kind of guy I'm used to. I guess being in the P.I.-slash-bodyguard business is perfect for you. Lets you exercise those overprotective muscles," she teased.

"Hmm."

They sat there in the dark, holding hands. She found it unbearably sweet. "Do bodyguards normally hold hands with their clients?"

"No. Well, I don't."

The finality in his voice pierced her. "There isn't going to be a you and me, is there?"

His gaze met hers. "Why do you ask?"

The rooms were cool and dark, and sitting with him holding her hand ranked as one of the most intimate things she'd ever done. She searched for the words to explain.

"It all feels like a fairy tale, you know? Cinderella finally goes to the ball, where she nabs the prince. Me, finally launching my career, and then an interesting, if slightly stuffy, guy comes along." She ran a finger down the tattooed names again. "I guess I'm wondering when the bubble will burst and reality will rear its ugly head. I mean, with any other guy, man, we'd already have done it and parted." She froze and her gaze darted to his face. "Wait. I'm not really as much a slut as that just made me sound."

"Already kicking me to the curb, and we haven't even slept together. I guess it's a good thing I don't get involved with clients." But laughter edged his voice, an intimate, easy sound, so Evie relaxed.

"Except you *are* involved with me." She tilted her chin up, daring him to deny it.

"I'm not the right guy for you, Evie. You need someone closer to your age, someone to make mistakes with. Grow old with. You want to know why I left the police force?"

"Uh, change of topic, but yeah, go ahead." She'd sit there and listen for hours.

He smiled. "It circles around, I promise. I met Marisa in college soon after my dad died. I thought we had everything in common. Six months later we married, and after we finished school, we went through the police academy together."

Shocked, Evie searched for something to say. Evie checked his arm again. "You're married? How come her name isn't on your arm? I would think your wife would be the person you'd protect the most. And give me props for not slugging you before I hear the facts."

She heard him catch his breath. "Was married, past tense. I don't know why she's not on my arm. I guess it didn't occur to me. Strange. Anyway, there was Marisa, right there beside me, going through academy training, taking the same exams. We cheered each other on, you know? Graduated together, went into the force together. We were put in separate divisions. Made sense. Three years into our time on the force, I find out she's having an affair with my partner. She swore it was all over, pledged her love to me, and I fell for it. Then one night, after we'd made love, she went into the kitchen, called 9-1-1 and claimed I'd raped her. Sobbed about her story all the way up the chain of command."

Shock held her for a moment. "The *bitch*. Why did she lie?" Fury and sadness churned inside her. "How devastating, to have the one person you should be able to trust above all others turn on you like that. I've had that, too. Totally sucks. But why did she do it?"

His hand tightened on hers. "No clue. It could have been ego, or a new boyfriend. She got what she wanted when I quit the force. She finally got fired when more of her lies came out. The divorce was not a pleasant one. I lost a lot of friends."

"God. I hope I never meet her, because I'd flatten her. And those people you called friends? They weren't, or you wouldn't have lost them."

His chuckle seemed a bit strained. "So to circle back around, I don't mix business with pleasure. Work and my private life are kept separate. It's better that way."

She frowned. Marisa. Beautiful name. Probably a beautiful woman. "That's like saying you'll never have a margarita again because tequila once gave you a hangover. Jake. All I'm asking for is a week. One lousy week, while we do this tour. We can stamp our own expiration date on the relationship. What's wrong with that?"

He shrugged. "Once bitten. So, who betrayed you?"

She jolted, her mood switching from concern for him to scared, that fast. "What do you mean? No one." She never told the story. Ever. Even though it was burned on her heart.

He cajoled. "Come on, Evie. You don't have to hide things from me. Who did you trust that turned on you?"

How did he know? She swallowed hard, but the lump in her throat didn't move. "Oh. That. I need a glass of water. Be right back."

***

Jake waited while Evie fled to the bathroom. Her empathy had soothed ugly feelings he hadn't realized were still there. If he could do that for her in return, then it would be a sleepless night well spent.

Her sleep clothes tonight were similar to the sunny yellow ones she'd worn the night before, slender pieces of silk, only this time they were a soft pink. Which was funny. In his opinion, she had a vibrant presence more suited to the vivid hues. Or was that merely her youthful energy?

He caught himself. It didn't matter. She was a client, and younger than his sisters. No more kissing. No more holding hands. He crossed his arms for good measure. No more, even though being with her came near to pure torture. Even though he'd love to take her up on her proposal of a week with no strings.

By the time she came back, he'd almost made peace with the fact that they weren't destined to be more than what they were now. Whatever that was.

"You're frowning. What's wrong?"

He shifted gears. "I'll never get used to your voice. It just kills me, every time. And I so didn't mean to say that."

She chuckled a little and sat so they faced each other. "That's very sweet of you, I think. So what's wrong?"

"Just life. You were going to tell me about that guy. When you were young. Who was he?"

Her chin went up. "Hm. I suppose if I said, just a guy, you'd keep pushing. But that's what you're gonna get."

"Okay. Skip that. Tell me the story of how you came to be a part of Mike's life."

She shot him a surprised look. "You don't know it?"

He knew some. "Mike told me bits and pieces. I'd like to hear it from you. If you're awake enough, that is." He leaned his head against the door and watched as her every thought flowed across her face.

"I'm wide awake." She sighed a little. "This is how it goes. Way back before I could think or walk or talk, I had a mama and a daddy. Then daddy left, I don't know why. Mama never said. And I grew older. Mama drank a lot. Did drugs. I kept growing and got put into school, somehow."

Her voice took on a singsong quality, as if reciting something she'd told a million times. Jake listened and watched her expressive face.

"One day, on the way home from school, some bullies were pushing me around, pushed me to the ground, taunting me. I was six, but even then I knew not to cry. A bigger boy came running, swinging his backpack at them, swearing in a loud voice. The bullies scattered. The boy—I'll call him B—helped me up from the ground, washed my knees off very gently, and walked me home. I never walked to or from school again by myself. He was always there."

She took a sip of water, continued her story. "He and his brother were foster kids with a family in my apartment complex. Everyone knew my mama was a drunk and an addict, but no one did anything. When she died, B helped me to hide so I wouldn't get taken away. His foster parents weren't the brightest people in the world, and they let me stay with them."

"That sounds nice."

She cast him a hard look. "It wasn't. I worked in their small restaurant every night after school in order to pay my way. The clothes I wore were hand-me-downs, always. School was pure torture. But B and his brother Ted were nice to me, in their way." She fell silent.

Jake let only a minute pass. "Then one day, you'd had enough, and you left," he supplied.

She picked up the thread. "And the next thing I knew, I was living with Mike. He pushed me to finish up my schooling. I got my GED, and then an AA in business. Plus everything else he taught me, about the music business." She spread her hands. "That's it. That's all. That's how it ends."

Jake couldn't let it go. There was more there. Had to be. "What happened to B?"

She shrugged. "He left me the year I turned fifteen. He and his brother took off to make their way in the world. I ran away, ran to the ocean. Lived there on and off for almost a year, until Mike took pity on me."

"So you became, in essence, a daughter to Mike," he said slowly.

"He was lonely. We'd seen each other before on the beach. One day, he heard me play a guitar that had a hole in it. I'd found it in the garbage in the neighborhood, rescued it, and took it to the beach with me. Tried to play it. I ended up begging one of the shopkeepers for some duct tape." She laughed then. "Not that the tape helped the sound a bit. It had been an amazing acoustic guitar, too—a Taylor. But someone had put his fist through the back of the wood."

He loved the mischief in her smile. "Let me guess. Mike?"

"Yeah. He got so mad when he heard me playing, too. Accused me of stealing it. He'd been drinking. Well, I just stood up to him, told him I'd found the guitar in the trash, and showed him the hole in the back and how I'd fixed it. When I told him I'd take far better care of it than he did, he went away."

Laughter lingered in her eyes, these memories chasing away the sad anger the earlier stories had brought. Jake smiled, picturing the scene. "What happened then?"

"He came back around sunset, sober finally, and found me still there struggling to remember chords. Making up my own and singing songs I'd written. He asked me what my situation was, and I told him. He took me to dinner at an outdoor taco stand that doesn't exist anymore, and we talked. He asked me to move in and I told him, no funny stuff. Well, he was shocked. He said he was old enough to be my grandfather which, of course, was true, but that wouldn't have stopped some guys."

"What convinced you to move in?"

Her eyes, swimming now with tears, met his. "He said he needed to teach me how to play properly. He said he was lonely, and wanted company, and he was getting too old to clean his house. He said he needed to get sober. He said he needed me, that he'd been waiting for someone just exactly like me to fill a hole in his life."

Jake's heart cracked at the sight of her pain. Despite his better judgment, he softened. "Come here." He opened his arms and she crept in, curled herself against him and cried. He just held her, rocked her, pressed kisses to hair that smelled of sunshine. Tears unmanned him when he was caught off guard. Everything about Evie seemed to catch him off guard, which had him baffled.

After several minutes, Evie's tears slowed.

"I miss him so much." She sniffled.

He rubbed her back. "I know. You should. You had ten years with him."

She laughed, hiccupped, and sighed. "He was such a b-brat. He never complained about feeling bad, just about not having a drink. I should have known earlier that he was sick."

"We went over this. He hated doctors, and he would have hated any pill taking. Don't beat yourself up because the man didn't get treatment in time."

She shifted away from him, wiped her runny nose with her wrist. "Oh God. I've slobbered all over your chest. Wait here."

She was back in a flash with a warm, wet washcloth. Jake just enjoyed her as she wiped his chest down, talking the entire time.

56

"I'm so embarrassed. I haven't sniveled like that in a long time. Tears are a weakness I can't afford. There, you're all clean now. So sorry." She took a hand towel and dried him off, her hands lingering.

"You can cry on me any time." Their gazes locked. The need in her eyes echoed a need he knew was growing inside him. But he tried to keep the pretense up. "You should get to bed. I promise you can sleep in for as long as you want."

She put the towel down. Her knees were right next to his hip, their mouths not far apart. "I just…" She took his face in her hands, leaned in, and took his breath away with the sweetness in her kiss.

Too much swirled between them during the brief meeting of lips and then she drew away. Gave him a shy smile. "Thank you. I'm exhausted now, so the crying did me some good." She picked up the wet washcloth and the hand towel and stood. "Sorry," she added over her shoulder.

Jake stood up, too, reaching out to tousle her hair. "Sleep well." He stepped back through the connecting door and shut it. He waited until she shut hers before he made his way in the dark room to the bed, shucked off his jeans, and tossed down onto the crisp sheets.

His body needed her like nobody's business. The feel of her hands on his chest had tightened every nerve he owned. All he could think of was ravishing her, of stripping those bits of silk off her body and feasting on the sweet flesh laid bare. Bringing her to an aching need until she begged for more. If she hadn't kissed him so sweetly, they might even now be rolling on the bed. His bed, her bed, it didn't matter. Right now, her idea of a week-long relationship sounded beyond good.

He cursed quietly and, completely torn, jumped out of bed and headed to the shower. The coldest he could stand. Maybe he'd missed his chance, or maybe his stuffy side was winning. Maybe she'd pulled back. Maybe he needed his head examined.

This was only the first night of the week-long tour. By the end of it, they'd either have explored this amazing connection between them, or he'd be a stark, raving lunatic.

CHAPTER SIX

The club seated no more than two hundred, in a dinner-theater style set of ascending terraces of booths and tables that faced a small stage. The place served drinks and appetizers. Canned music played softly in the background.

Evie watched from near the club entrance as the band set up, her stomach in knots. The place was about half full. The club manager had told her the day before that the late show grabbed a bigger audience, which totally worked for her. It would give her time to lose her nerves. As it was past ten p.m., they were running late, but she was fine with that, too. She'd always been a night owl. Her next show would be at midnight.

It was too bad that Conway couldn't have been there tonight. At least he'd said he was working on another, longer tour for her. She'd take it. Anything for the experience at this point.

Jake stood nearby, doing his bodyguard impression by wearing a dark suit and keeping his arms crossed. The scowl on his handsome face made him even more unapproachable, but seeing him like that relaxed her. Let her know all was well, since he was there.

It was like having Mike around, only different. Same protective vibe, but she'd never wanted to jump Mike's bones. Don't go there, girl. Distraction, distraction. Songs, that was it.

Mentally, she ran through the song list for that night. They were doing some oldies, a couple of Mike's songs, and two of hers unless she chickened out. The band would follow her lead. Whatever she said tonight they'd do, and they'd discuss how it flowed tomorrow over a late breakfast.

Oh God. She never should have thought of food. Pressing a hand to her stomach, her panic grew, as did her nausea. She fled to the small door at the back, ducked into the kitchen and bent over a trashcan. Vomited.

A worker shouted at her. She vomited again, the bile burning her throat. A kind hand thrust a glass of water toward her. She rinsed her mouth and spit the water out into the trashcan.

The waitress shoved a paper towel in her hand. "Wipe out your mouth then have another sip of water. Then get out there. You can do it, honey. I heard you practice earlier."

Evie heard the manager giving her a brief intro. A smattering of applause was quickly drowned out by the band playing the opening bars of "St. James Infirmary."

"Oh God." she rinsed out her mouth once more.

The waitress patted her on the back and took the glass of water. "Go!"

She went. Pushed out the door, strutted down the aisle to the stage. Bear winked at her. She turned, picked up the hand-held microphone resting on the stool, and launched into the song with her best growly belt voice. Usually a man sang "St. James Infirmary," but tonight she made the song of New Orleans all her own.

The applause was enthusiastic, so she dove right into the next song without taking a break, loving every minute of being up there, connecting with the audience. As "House of the Rising Sun" wound down, this time she took a break and let them applaud, laughing and bowing.

"Thank you, all of you, thanks very much," she said. "I need to introduce my band. The most wonderful people on God's green earth, I love them all. Please meet sweet Reid Farmer, rocking on bass guitar. Jimmy Lewis working his magic on keyboards, and the fabulous Bear Jones on drums." She paused as the band received their applause, bowing and blowing her kisses.

She took a couple sips of water, then settled the microphone in the stand and picked up her guitar. "Okay, I'm gonna change things up now, and do a couple of tunes by Mike Harper. My friend and mentor, gone too soon. But he wrote this little ditty, and gave me the privilege of being the first to sing it. We recorded it as a duet a couple of years ago, and you can still find it on his website. Unfortunately, we never got to sing it in front of an audience. It's called *Baby Girl Bad*."

She sat on the stool and played a lively tune, the band silent behind her, waiting for their cue to begin.

"Baby girl came running/Oh baby girl she cry/Bullies they beat down/On the pride of Daddy's eye/Her daddy came out swinging/But a bully had a gun/Baby's all alone now/And Baby's on the run/Don't cry for Baby, brought up to hold a grudge/She's gunning for them bullies and Baby ain't gonna budge. Baby girl bad…"

***

Jake couldn't take his eyes off Evie. That voice, killer when she spoke, dug into his gut and churned there when she sang. A quick glance around the audience told him they were feeling it, too. She finished the song and the applause was thunderous. On cue, she dashed off stage for a costume change while the band continued to play a medley of Mike's hits.

When she returned, she wore the dress his sister had made for her, the one that made him think of the ocean, still with those mile-high heels showing off her great legs. She had done something different with her hair, and instead of a mop of curls, she looked like a forties torch singer. He had to admit he liked it.

She swung into a rock anthem of Mike's next, one that spoke of summer nights and beer and whatever-happened-to, a song of a love that never lasted. This one had stayed on the top of the charts for almost a year a couple of decades ago. Had been a part of his life playlist for many years.

As she sang, his growing need for her sank deep inside him. She was like a drug he'd been resisting. Was he too stuffy? It wasn't like she'd set a wedding date and picked out a white dress that looked good from the back.

It was just sex.

Something they both needed. They were adults. And her idea of a week-long affair had convinced him she could handle it.

As he watched her mesmerize the audience, all his good intentions about keeping his hands off her slid away and hunger roared through him. How long until he could get her to himself?

A tap on the shoulder pulled him back to reality. The front desk manager beckoned him out the door.

Jake followed.

"My apologies, sir, but you wanted to be informed whenever anyone left anything for Ms. Marcherand. This just came for her." The manager handed him an envelope with Evie's name on it. Jake took it.

"Any ID on the messenger?"

The manager shook his head. "Nothing. I turned my back, went to the printer to get a customer's receipt, you know? Came back and it was sitting on my desk. The customer said he was absorbed in his cell phone, and he didn't see who left it either. We can check the surveillance footage, but it will have to wait until tomorrow as I've got a skeleton staff tonight."

Damn it. Jake sighed. "Thank you. As soon as you have anything from the cameras, let me know." He tipped the manager, and inspiration struck. "I'd like to change rooms to a suite, as far from our existing rooms as possible. Plus champagne." He passed another bill, this one a hundred, to the manager. "If you can have everything moved before the second show ends?"

The manager smiled. "Absolutely. I'll be back with the new cardkeys before she starts her second set." The manager went off, whistling slightly under his breath.

Jake opened the envelope, pulled out another letter looking like the first one, this time with slightly more inventive threats. So their stalker *had* followed them. Perfect. Just fucking perfect. He stuffed the note back in the envelope and put it in his pocket.

The arrangements he'd just made to change their room situation eased his mind, and he'd be in touch with the police in the morning after he viewed the surveillance tape. Nothing else he could do about it tonight but keep her safe. Much easier to do if they shared a bed. Anticipation fizzed in his veins and he shoved his hands into his pockets. Told himself to calm down. There were at least a couple of hours to get through before he could get her alone.

He slipped back into the club.

Evie had gone on to another song, something terribly romantic, but Jake had been pulled out of her spell, jerked back to reality. Instead of focusing on her, he checked out the patrons, something he should have been doing all along. There were two entrances to the club and while no one had passed him, latecomers could easily have gone in the other entrance.

Frustratingly, all the people in the club looked normal. You had your typical newlyweds of all ages, long-married couples, the just-twenty-one-ers. Gay couples, straight couples, interracial couples. No one sat alone, nursing a whiskey and casting brooding glances at the stage. On the contrary, Evie had them all rocking and having a great time.

Hell. Even the waitresses were typical of any Vegas casino.

He moved across the back and checked everyone out from the other angle but didn't have any new bright ideas. No revelations.

Jake watched the audience, and Evie, for the rest of the set. Sixty minutes had never seemed so long. When she'd finally said "thank you and good night, everybody" he was more than ready to whisk her off between sets, just like they'd planned. Anything to keep her safe.

As the patrons streamed toward the exits, Jake waded against the tide to reach the stage. Evie was chatting with a young couple, and, laughing happily, she signed their ticket to her show. The woman squealed and kissed her man and they turned and left. She saw Jake, and her face lit up with a happy expectation.

Jake stepped between her and the front of the stage, his urge to protect growing stronger at the slight chaos behind him. "Time to go. Are you going to change, or wear what you've got on?"

Evie's megawatt smile dimmed. "Change. I'll be right back. You know, there's no way out of this place except through those front doors, so you don't have to follow me." She tossed her head and turned on her heel. Stomped off stage.

Damn it. Jake put his hands on his hips, baffled, and tried to catch the eye of one of the band. They, however, studiously ignored him as they wiped down instruments. "What did I say? Come on, guys."

Reid and Jimmy just shrugged. Bear ambled toward him, an amiable giant of a man. "You pissed her off, wanting to hustle her out of here."

"I had my reasons." Still, he frowned.

Bear favored him with a long look. "Son. You didn't congratulate her. You didn't tell her she was awesome. You didn't tell her how beautiful she looked tonight, how killer she sounded. Instead, you treated her like a child to be bundled inside because she'd played too long out in the rain."

"I followed you until the last part," Jake said, only slightly amused.

"Hell, you know what I mean. What's going on? Why are you so jittery?"

At Bear's words, the other two men stopped to listen.

Jake didn't hesitate, but moved toward them and kept his voice down. "We've got a stalker. Keep your mouth shut about it, but keep your eyes on her when I'm not around, okay? Someone out there doesn't want Baby to sing."

"And you want to keep Baby in the dark." Bear frowned his disapproval.

"It was Mike's idea to keep her in the dark. Hard not to agree with him."

"I don't like that part, and I don't agree, but we know how protective Mike was, so we'll do as you've asked. For now." Bear nodded, a hard glint in his eye.

"I appreciate it. The more eyes on the crowds, the better off we'll all be."

Bear didn't answer, just headed back to his drums. "Men, shall we hit the slots? We've got a whole forty-five minutes until our next set."

"I'm game." They saluted Jake as they went past, leaving just him and the busboys clearing off the tables for the next show.

***

Evie fumed as she slipped out of her dress and into the long silk shirt in a deep pink. Next came the pair of designer jeans she'd kept ready. She pulled a couple of pins out of her hair and shook her head, fluffed her curls until they were her usual style.

She'd wanted him to tell her she was fabulous. He was supposed to say she was the next bright star in the music industry, guaranteed Grammys. What did he say? "Time to go." As if he'd been wasting his time listening.

Damn it. She'd thought they'd made huge strides last night, talking in the dark, getting him over some of his in-born stuffiness. And as much as she'd wanted to discover everything about him, now she thought that maybe he was right, and he was really too old for her. Too set in his ways. Too—stuffy.

She brooded as she looked at herself in the dimly lit mirror. The dressing room was smaller than some broom closets, with only one hard wooden chair and a tiny dressing table, but she had no complaints. Unless they were about Jake's attitude.

With one last sigh, she tucked her room key into the rear pocket of her jeans and headed out, still wearing the heels she'd had on for the last outfit. This was Las Vegas. It was time she had some fun.

She found Jake prowling around the stage, peering out into the audience. With the stage lights off and the people cleared out, the place looked kind of sad. Like it was waiting. Well, she was done waiting. It was time to do some living.

"I'm ready for the slot machines. What do you think?" She tilted her chin and dared him to argue.

He took her in, all of her, from her curls to her heels. Peered into her eyes, where she was sure he saw thunderbolts. She waited, tense, for him to refuse.

"Slot machines. That's where the guys went," he said. "Shall we?" To her surprise, he held out an arm for her.

She took it. Sniffed. "I can walk, you know."

"I know. You strutted in heels on the stage for an hour, and you did a top-notch job. I'm just here for you to lean on. And so I can smell you," he said, dipping his nose down toward her ear. "Mm. You smell like success."

She didn't know whether to scoff at him, slap him, or grin, so she did nothing. Keeping her face bored as they came out of the club and into the casino proper, she arched an eyebrow up at him. "And what does success smell like, pray tell?" There was no way she'd admit that she'd vomited before her first song.

A smile tugged at his lips, those thin, mobile lips that knew how to kiss her senseless, and for a moment everything seemed right in her world.

"That's for me to know, and you to find out," he whispered in her ear as he steered her toward the slot machines.

A shiver of appreciation worked its way down her back, tightened her nipples. "Oh, and I will find out, trust me."

"I'm counting on it," he drawled. He stopped in the middle of the machines. "What's your pleasure?"

She bit her lip at the amusement and awareness mingled in his eyes. "Why, Jake Wells, whatever do you mean?"

"Nickel, dime, quarter, dollar slots, ma'am? Or something—richer? More interesting, you might say?"

She could feel her panties grow wet at the suggestion in his voice. "Let's start with the quarter slots. Maybe after my second show I can afford to try something richer and, ah, more interesting," she said, and, passing him, she trailed her fingers across his chest. Tugged at his tie to make sure he followed as she picked out just the right quarter machine.

Settling at one with sevens and diamonds, she dug a twenty out of her pocket. "I've been saving it for the slots," she said, feeding the bill into the machine with a happy little dance on the stool. "Are you going to play?"

He sent her a smoldering look. "I'll watch you now and play later. It'll be more fun that way."

Evie snickered. "Who are you, and what have you done with Mister Stuffy Pants?"

"Trust me, I don't stuff my pants. No need."

"And now you're bragging," she mused as she punched the button on the machine. "I'll be happy to play later, as long as I get some say in the play," she murmured, heat from his gaze warming her.

He barked a short laugh. "I wouldn't have it any other way. I was thinking that expiration date you mentioned isn't that far away, and we've wasted time."

Desire, never far away lately, burst through her in a rush at his words.

She arched an eyebrow. "You mean, you wasted time."

"Yeah, okay. I wasted time. Well? Are you going to play that machine, or just stare at me?"

She took a breath and turned away from him. It took all her concentration to sit and play with the twenty she'd allotted herself, even as she wondered what had happened to change his mind.

Wondered what kind of play he preferred.

That thought had her eyes glazing and she hit the button with slightly more vigor than she had before. The numbers and diamonds rolled, until three pretty white sevens lined up in a row and the machine began to jingle.

Evie blinked. "Did I win?"

"You did. Two hundred coins. Fifty bucks. Congratulations, you've more than doubled your money. Walk away now while you still have it," he added.

She looked down expectantly at the tray, but nothing came out. "Where is it? I want my quarters." She banged the machine lightly. Stupid machine, keeping her money.

"If you're ready to go back to the club, just push the cash-out button and you'll get a voucher for the money."

"Oh." She sent Jake a sheepish look. "They don't show it like that in the movies."

"I know. Things have changed in the gaming industry. Nowhere near as much fun as it used to be, in my opinion. Come on; let's get you back to the club to get ready."

She punched the cash out button and sure enough, a receipt came out. "I can cash this, right? Should I do it now?" She waved it at him.

"Why don't you do it later?" He glanced at his watch. "You've got about fifteen minutes before the show is supposed to start, though we both know it'll go up ten minutes late."

"True. But you're right. Let's get back to the club." She stood, making sure to brush against him as she passed. She sent him a wicked look. "The sooner the performance is done, the sooner I can get to, oh, what did you call it? Richer entertainment. I am so looking forward to it," she added, slipping her arm through his. "Fab suggestion of yours." Her breasts ached, so she pressed close to his side as they walked, and was rewarded by Jake's sharp intake of breath.

Nerves fluttered in her belly. She felt absolutely lit up and glowy inside. Work ahead that she loved, and a man to—explore, that was a good word for it. Man, she loved her life. Couldn't get any better. As long as her nerves left her stomach alone, she'd be just fine.

CHAPTER SEVEN

"I thought the second set went really well. The audience was much more sober than I had expected," Evie said as they walked through the casino. If she just kept talking, she'd avoid the nerves that had attacked the minute she'd stepped offstage. A different type of stage fright. "What did you think? Of course, maybe I was just too jazzed to see how drunk they really were."

She had her dresses and jeans over one arm, not trusting the management to keep them safe overnight. Jake's hand rested, hot and heavy, against her back. It burned through the red dress she'd put back on. Jake didn't say a word, just kept scanning the casino. She tried again.

"A packed house, too. Oh, and did you see the cute couple up front? I sang happy anniversary to them, though I was surprised they were only on their second anniversary. They had to be over seventy at least. Oh man, I'm starving. Dinner was a long time ago—want to get something to eat?" She chanced another glance up at Jake. His face was set, and possessiveness lingered in his eyes.

"Later."

It was all he said, but a thrill went through her. The stuffy Jake was gone, as was the flirty, suggestive Jake from earlier. In his place was dangerous, sexy Jake from the beach. She'd take the time with him and not look any further.

Because planning ahead, planning for the future, always led to disaster. Better to stick to the here and now, and their agreed-upon expiration date. When the tour was over, they were over. That just kept everything neat and tidy, she assured herself. She had recordings to do. Maybe another club tour. A career to manage, and all that. She'd be fine on her own, without anyone to lean on. It was time to learn that again.

They reached the elevator just as it opened. The people waiting ahead of them entered, then Jake. The only place left was directly in front of him. She stood, her back against his front. Jake used the opportunity to pull her hips back against him, his erection tight against her. She closed her eyes. Her body throbbed. They rode in silence up to the sixth floor, where everyone exited except for them.

The elevator doors slid shut, closing them in together. Jake had moved back against the rear. She turned, caught the hungry look on his face. They stared at each other, primal need holding them silent as the elevator rose silently, passing the tenth floor and on up to the twelfth before coming to a stop.

On a quick gasp of breath, Evie exited and stopped in the elevator lobby. Jake came up behind her, his hand once again on her back before he smoothed it down over the slight curve of her ass. She shivered and looked up at him.

"This is stupid, but I don't remember which way to go." Her voice wobbled. "Wait. I thought we were on the tenth floor?"

He turned her toward the left and they walked, Jake still not saying a word. "I don't recognize any of this."

Jake kept walking. "You can go back to the room on the tenth floor if you want, later. But tonight, I want you to share a suite with me."

He stopped at the end of the hallway and used the cardkey for entrance. Pushed open the door. "Ladies first."

Evie entered, her astonishment growing as she looked around. The room was easily three times the size of hers and furnished with an elegance she'd never known. A huge window covered the far wall, looking out over the sparkling lights of the Las Vegas Strip. Candles were lit along the wide windowsill. A round table for two, set with a white cloth, carried a bud vase with one long-stemmed red rose. To the right was a formal sitting area, with wing chairs and a sofa covered in striped silk, and a gas fireplace. Off to the left, a door led to a bedroom where a king-sized bed shimmered white in the night, and roses sat on the night table. The suite smelled like roses and vanilla and moonlight.

Emotion clogged her throat and the clothes in her arms fell to the floor as she stared. This was too much. This was borderline romantic, and she was the daughter of a drug addict. Oh, God. This wasn't her world. What the hell was she doing here?

Jake let out a strained chuckle. "I guess you like it."

Evie clutched her throat. "I can't breathe." She bent over, gasping for air, panic stricken. "Jake, I can't breathe. This is too much. Too rich. I can't…I don't belong here. You didn't have to…"

A knock on the door had her standing fast. Too fast. Her head spun and she staggered.

The knock came again. "Room service."

Jake cursed and grasped her arms to steady her. "Don't move," he ordered, and he went to the door. A waiter entered, moving a rolling cart smoothly to the table by the window.

Evie bolted for the door to the bathroom, only to find herself in a closet. "Damn it." Panic lined her stomach, made it slick. "Where's the bathroom?" She came out of the closet to find the next door over, held open by Jake. "Thank you," and she pulled the door closed, locked it, and slumped against it, staring at the gruesome object opposite.

Her image in the mirror. Big glassy eyes, clownish red lips.

Panic had left a fine sheen of sweat on her face. Not exactly the plan for this part of the evening. Just breathe, damn it. Closing her eyes, she took it slow, allowing herself to relax against the door. Kicking off the sky-high heels helped. Looking around at the luxury in the bathroom didn't help, so she confined herself to grabbing a face towel and carefully blotting the sweat off.

All she managed to accomplish was smear her mascara and make one edge of her eyelashes all wonky. Damn. Who was she trying to kid, anyway? With a sigh, she peeled off the false eyelashes. She reached for some fancy jar of cream, and proceeded to cleanse the evening's work from her face.

After a cool splash of water and another, more vigorous rub with the towel, she had regained her sense of humor.

"You okay, Evie?"

A concerned Jake. She opened the door, leaned against the doorjamb and gave him a rueful smile. "Sorry. I hope I haven't ruined your evening."

"Couldn't happen." He tilted her chin up, scrutinized her face. "You know, on stage that makeup really works for you. But up close and personal?" He bent down, gave her a light kiss. "I much prefer you this way."

Cursing the way her heart jumped, she fought to keep her hand steady as she brushed it down his chest, noting his tee shirt and jeans. "You changed. Do you mind if I change, too?"

He drew back, grinned. "What color are your jammies tonight?"

Heat flooded her cheeks. "I have to go to my room. I don't remember what I brought with me."

"Don't hate me. I had all of our things moved to this room."

"Ah." She took refuge in nibbling on her fingernail before pulling her hand away from her mouth, embarrassed.

Jake didn't seem to notice. He walked backwards into the room, holding a hand out to her. "I've got champagne. Would you like a glass?"

Evie pursed her lips, took a couple steps into the suite, put her hand into his waiting one. A sitting area to her right, the bedroom with its huge bed to the left. In front of her, the window, the candles, the table now set with covered dishes. An ice bucket, keeping a bottle cold.

"I don't know. I've never had champagne." She took a deep breath. Such a different world from where she'd began. "Yes. Open that bottle, and I'll change."

She headed to the bedroom, poked around in the drawers, she grabbed what she needed and whisked back into the bathroom. Turned the shower on to hot and stripped off the red dress. A quick wash and rinse later, she pulled on her silk nightie and took a breath. Smoothed her hair back from her face and grimaced at her reflection. "Here goes nothing."

***

Jake looked out over the city, wondering if he'd gone too far with the expensive room, the food, the champagne. For all the glory she'd shown on stage tonight, he had to remember she was more like the girl on the beach. Sexy, yes, and all woman, but not used to luxury, or a man treating her like a goddess. But the most recent threat worried him, and keeping her close and in a room—with him—seemed to be the best option.

Plus he was tired of putting up arbitrary barriers to something he truly wanted.

The bathroom door opened and he turned. Caught his breath. She came toward him through the dimly lit room, shy yet with laughter lingering in her expressive eyes. The silk she wore was the same siren red as the dress that she tossed toward the closet, but more like a slip with tiny straps, the flared skirt flirting with her upper thighs.

"It needs cleaning. The dress."

"I'll take care of it in the morning." He lifted a crystal flute, passed it to her, picked up his own, and tapped her glass. "Congratulations on a stunning debut. You rocked the house, Evie."

She seemed to glow from the inside, her smile splitting her face in two. "Thanks." She took a sip, licked her lips. Lifted the glass to stare at the liquid inside. "It's amazing. Like tiny stars swimming in the ocean. Little bubbles of happy." She turned in a circle, taking it all in again. "And this room, wow. Just, wow. What are you, a gazillionaire?"

He smiled. "I called in a favor from a friend, to help you celebrate. You like it? I don't need to move us back to the other rooms?"

"No. I mean, yes, I love it. Thank you for making this night so special." She sipped again, set the glass down. "Now I need you to make it a little more special." She took his glass from him, set it next to her own.

"How?" The need that had dogged him since he first saw her under the moonlight grew stronger as she set her hands to his tee shirt. His answer came as she lifted it up over his head. He finished the job, stripping it off. It landed somewhere behind them.

"No more nerves?" He fingered the silky strands of her hair as she stepped closer to him. She had been seriously adorable in her panic earlier, but now she looked like a woman on a mission.

She spread her hands across his chest, sending ripples of want through him, and tilted her head up to him. "None. You?"

"No nerves here." He had to give her a chance to back away. "Are you sure this is what you want? Because I'm done with keeping my hands off you."

"Were you the man I kissed in the moonlight? Wearing a suit on the beach?" She went up on tiptoe, tracing his torso up to his shoulders, where she clung. "Kiss me again. Please. Haven't we wasted enough time?"

Heart in his throat, he pulled her to him and kissed her. And just like on the beach, her hands speared into his hair, and after the first passionate meeting of lips, it changed into something more. Something deeper.

Jake swept her up and she wrapped her legs around his waist, clasped her hands around his neck as he carried her to the bedroom and the rose-petal-strewn bed. He set her on it and followed her down, catching her lips with his.

Lost. He got lost in her, in her taste, her scent, the feel of her body beneath him. This woman had gotten under his guard so fast it still made his head spin. Her lips were soft, yet demanding. Her body stretched beneath his.

Her hands sparked fires across his skin, wherever she touched. Her legs twined with his even as her hands brushed between them, searching for the button on his jeans.

She broke from their kiss with a gasp. "Get these damned things off. Now."

He pushed away and stood, ripping the buttons open with one yank. Shucked the jeans down and stepped out of them, aware that her gaze had gone straight to his erect cock. He climbed on the bed, intent on her.

"Don't move," he said, and started at her foot. He caressed the high arch, her toes. The narrow heel, and on up. Her calf. Her skin was soft, smooth, pale. Fragrant. He stopped when he got to the red silk hem. Kissed her there, on her thigh. Breathed deep.

She smelled of roses and perfume and woman. Intoxicating.

"Jake, so help me." The words came out on a strangled sigh. "I need you."

"I'm in no hurry. We've got all night." He nudged the silk up, higher, pushed it up to her belly. No panties. Her sex, barely covered with blonde curls, glistened as she moved restlessly beneath him. Beautiful. He inhaled.

"I love the way you smell, the way you feel. You are beautiful." He kissed her sharp little hipbone, slid his tongue across her belly to her navel. Suckled there, teeth and tongue teasing her.

She gasped. Grabbed his hand and put it on her breast. "You're driving me crazy here."

"That's the idea." He squeezed gently, flicked the nipple that had come to life beneath his palm before releasing her and sitting up. He tugged at the silk. "Off."

She laughed, grabbed it by the hem, and pulled it off over her head, flinging it aside where it pooled, dark against the snowy-white coverlet. She reached for him.

"Not yet. Just lay back and let me look at you." He watched as she did so, her dark eyes beckoning him. Her full lips pouted a little, begging him to kiss her without a word.

Her body lay bare in front of him, just as he'd fantasized. Her muscles were lean, slender, her body in perfect proportion, and a part of him kicked himself for not following her that night on the beach for hot and frenzied sex. They'd moved beyond that stage now. Now, he wanted to cherish her. Show her how much he cared. He didn't know how. Wasn't sure he'd ever known how.

Evie waited, anticipation winding her up. She watched him as he sat on his heels at the foot of the bed, taking inventory of her. The heavy muscles of his chest made her fingers itch to touch. His healthy erection had her licking her lips. Him watching her made her feel crazy-sexy. She could feel her sex growing wetter and plump and ready for him.

"Since you're just watching, I'll give you something to see." She set her hands to her stomach, brought them slowly up to her breasts. She cupped them, tugged and then rolled her nipples, and gasped at the sensation. Did it again, arched her back as her arousal added to the scents in the air.

Jake's eyes gleamed as he watched.

"I'm not a child, Jake." She rolled her hips toward him invitingly.

"I never thought you were."

"I want you. I want you deep inside me. I want to scream out my release in your arms. I want to give you such pleasure that you'll be drunk on it for a week."

He touched her then, as before, starting at her foot and stroking up to her hip, slid over her stomach and down to her sex. She parted her legs. He petted her, combed his fingers through her curls, not yet dipping into her wetness. Evie let out a little whimper.

"What do you like? Do you like this?" He moved one finger to her inner lips. "You're so wet." He slid a finger into her and she moaned. "Like that?"

"More. Damn it, Jake. I've wanted you. I need you, so bad."

He didn't say anything, just eased a second finger into her. With his thumb barely brushing her clit, he started slowly moving his fingers in and out.

She gasped, her hands falling to her sides. Her need rose fast now, her eyes almost blind with pleasure.

"Put your hands back on your breasts. I want you to tug on your nipples, Evie. Give me a show, and I promise you'll come."

Evie tugged and pulled on her nipples. Pinched and rolled and moaned as the heat in her breasts seemed directly connected to the heat between her legs. Her hips moved and Jake caught her rhythm.

"You are so beautiful," he said. "Scream for me, Evie. Scream." He lightly pinched her clit while plunging his fingers into her.

Evie screamed, the orgasm rushing through her, shaking her body. Even as she eased, little firestorms of energy sparked off her body here and there. Her arms fell to her sides. Jake slid his fingers out of her, caressed her clit once more. She jumped in response.

"You're not done yet, are you?"

She lifted her head, smiled at him. "Not at all. Just, ah, resting."

He pressed kisses across her slight belly, down to where her scent called him. He settled himself between her thighs, spread them wide, and tasted her, sweet and tart and totally Evie. He set himself to tease.

Evie jumped at the first lick. She gripped his shoulders. "Jake. Please."

"Let me." He bent his head to her again. She struggled to breathe under his gentle assault, his tongue and fingers toying with her, playing in her wetness, driving her up and up. Her body tightened, and he backed off, pressing nipping kisses along the inside of her thighs until she'd relaxed, not quite reaching the peak. He set his mouth to her again, his fingers, bringing her to just the edge before backing off again.

She let out a shuddering sigh as her muscles went lax. "I hate you."

"Mmm," he agreed. Licked her, one long swipe of his tongue. "I'm loving this, though." He suckled.

Her strangled cry was his reward. He kept licking her, suckling, until the shudders left her body and she went limp beneath his hands.

He moved up, took her in his arms and just held her close.

"You are. Man." In the dark, her killer voice seemed huskier than ever. Sleepy. "I've never."

Pride grew inside him. "Never what?"

"Never quite like that." She sighed and turned into him, her hand finding his still-hard cock. He sighed in relief as she played with him. "You didn't think I was going to ignore you, did you?"

"Mm. I thought that maybe you were going to take a quick nap." He pressed a kiss on her head.

"Not sleepy." She rose up over him, pushed him back against the bed. She gleamed pink and gold and white, a fantasy come true, and he found himself gripped with anticipation. He brought his hands to her breasts and for a second she leaned into him, let him learn her, mold her, tease her reddened nipples. She shivered in pleasure before moving out of his reach.

"Hands above your head. No touching," she added, a wicked glint in her eyes. "Think you can handle it?"

The chuckle died in his throat as her fingers did the walking. "I think so."

"Good. Before I forget, where are the condoms?" Her hand squeezed his cock, released.

"Bedside table," he got out.

"Don't move," she said, and climbed over him to get to the drawer.

He breathed her in. Swiped her sweet ass with his tongue and bit down gently, grinning when she yelped and moved that part of her anatomy hastily out of his reach.

"You put it where I can touch, and I will," he said. A couple foil packets landed near him as she scrambled away from his mouth.

"Not right now," she scolded. "It's my turn."

Jake closed his eyes. Warm air blew across the head of his cock before the warm wetness of her mouth descended. Took him all in, before retreating. Once more, with her tongue doing a swirly thing at the tip. Then again, and again. Dear God, she was good at this.

She took him to the edge before stopping. The sensation of her fingers never left him as she sheathed him, first in the condom, then in her body. He opened his eyes. She sat there, his cock deep inside her, looking like a wicked wanton with her hands once again on her breasts.

She sighed in relief and began to move. He let her have her way for several seconds before rolling her beneath him.

"Evie." he smoothed the hair out of her eyes, uncertain as to what to say. "I need you."

She looked up at him, a smile in her eyes. She tilted her hips, wrapping her legs and tightening her muscles around him. "Then take me. Take me with you."

He kissed her then and drove inside her welcoming body. The heat, the tightness, the scent of the two of them had his heart thundering. He could feel her pulse beating in time with his. He wanted to go slow. Wanted to take his time, to enjoy the mewling sounds coming from her, enjoy the slick hotness of her body. Revel in the feel of her hands on him, stroking him, urging him, her nails digging into his ass and hanging on.

He bent down to take her nipple into his mouth and suckled, desperate to hold off just a bit longer. Her body gripped his and she cried out as she came, triggering his orgasm. Their cries blended in the night as release shook them both.

Evie sank into the bed, boneless, weighted down by Jake who was breathing heavily, resting on his elbows above her. His forehead dropped to hers and he kissed her, a lingering, lovely kiss. She touched his cheek, ran her fingers over his lips when they parted. He nuzzled her throat.

"So damned sexy," he murmured.

She closed her eyes, smiled. Felt his kiss on her shoulder before he slipped out of her. Kissed her again.

"I'll be back in a minute."

"I'll be here."

She floated, her mind incapable of handling anything other than reliving what they had just done, her body still buzzing with mini explosions. Faster than she'd thought possible he'd returned, tugged the covers she was still sprawled on down from under her, then crawled in beside her. He drew the covers up around them and snugged her to him.

It felt strange. Different. She breathed him in, delighted in the hair-covered skin brushing against hers. Reveled in the heavy weight of his arm across her waist, his legs tangled with hers, her bottom snug against him.

"Jake?"

"Hm?"

"I really like you."

His chest quaked behind her and she slapped his hand. "Stop laughing," but she laughed with him. "I don't know why I said that."

"You only like me because I just gave you multiple orgasms."

She joined in again on his laughter. "Well, duh. That's definitely in the equation."

His chuckles subsided and he kissed her bare shoulder. "I really like you, too. What do you think about saving on space, and sharing a room for the rest of the tour?"

"I think that sounds about perfect." Her tummy rumbled. "Are you sleepy?"

"Nope. Hungry?"

"Yep. Plus I haven't finished drinking my bubbles of happy," she said, and turned in his arms to frame his face. Gave him a smacking kiss. "You make me happy. It's a night of surprises. Let's get up," and she slipped from his side, found her red gown, and slipped it on.

He grabbed her around the waist and she shrieked, laughed as he pulled her down for a kiss. "So that's it? You fuck me and then leave me for bubbles and food?"

"I'd much rather take you with me," she said, kissing him back. "Or we could bring the food and bubbles here, and feed each other." She arched a brow. "What do you say?"

"Race you to the table." He was on his feet faster than she could find the edge of the bed.

"I can't walk yet, much less run." She watched, laughing, as he sprinted for the champagne. "Don't go too fast, or you'll spill it."

He turned, champagne glasses in hand. "I will be happy to serve you, my lady." He brought the glasses over and handed her one. "To you." They tapped glasses and drank. "I'll be right back."

She arranged the pillows high against the headboard and watched with interest as a naked Jake, his body strong, tan and gleaming in the candlelight, carried first the standing ice bucket and then a plate of food to the bed. He climbed in next to her.

"I wasn't sure what you'd like, so I got cheese and strawberries and salami and crackers."

"Perfect." She sighed happily as she bit into the strawberry he held out for her. The flavor burst on her tongue. "Oh man. So good."

"Yes." He kissed her, smoothed her hair. "You are. So good." He grinned and her eyebrows rose.

"What's so funny?" She layered a slice of cheese with a piece of salami on top of a cracker and bit in.

"You. Running into the closet. Hysterical." And he laughed.

She smacked him on the arm even as she laughed too. "I know. Weird. I don't get panic attacks. Well, I did when Brad ran out on me." She stopped abruptly. Drank down her champagne. "Refill, please."

"Brad? Was he the one who left you when you were fifteen?" Jake refilled her glass and returned the bottle to the ice bucket.

Evie took time to chew her snack, thinking fast. Did it matter at this point? Surely no one could possibly care. She swallowed, sipped champagne and leaned against the pillows with a sigh. Maybe it was time to pull the stinger out. "Bradley Gaines." She watched as Jake assimilated the information, but his face didn't change.

"The pop star turned country?"

"Mm. We were going to take the world by storm with our act. My songwriting, our singing together. We had it all planned when we were ten and twelve. Then, somewhere along the line, the dream changed, became all about his career. Then he and his brother Ted just left. They walked away and left me with a couple that only cared how much I could help them out at the restaurant. They left me behind." Even now the thought was shaming. She hadn't been good enough.

"The bastard." Cold fury infused the words.

She found she could smile then. Patted his hand. "You're a good man, Jake Wells."

"Not all men are like him, you know." He twisted around to look her in the eyes. "Most men aren't like him."

"I know." She cupped his face between her hands, kissing him gently. "Mike has introduced me to many men who are nothing like Brad. Then there's you, a different breed altogether."

He wrapped an arm around her, brought her against his chest. She nestled there, content, hearing the beat of his heart, enjoying the feel of his other hand in her hair.

"I'm glad we've got this little bit of time together. I can't imagine all the other jobs you've put off in order to babysit me like this. Mike must have paid you well." She lifted her head, stricken. "Hell. I didn't mean that the way it sounded."

He chuckled. "I'm not offended, and I know what you meant."

She settled again. "Brad's been on my mind a lot lately. He got his start here in Vegas, you know. Pass me a strawberry?"

He held one out for her to nibble.

"I've never eaten strawberries in bed before."

"It may be the first time, but I'm sure it won't be the last. You've got a lot of talent, Evie. You've got a long career ahead of you."

"Hm. I like to think so. As long as I can sing, right? Or write songs." She sipped at her champagne and sighed happily. "I'm so glad you're here. If you weren't, I'd be feeling really lonely right now. I'd probably be in the casino losing money and getting plowed on the free drinks at the slot machines."

"I'm glad I'm here, too."

She tipped her head to look into his eyes. "So, you're not upset that you aren't in France, instead?"

"Let me think. Uh, no. There isn't a place I'd rather be than right here, in this bed, with you."

"We can go to the Paris Hotel tomorrow, if you want. Take our picture in front of the Eiffel Tower and pretend." Evie yawned, covered her mouth and giggled. "Sorry. I think I'm finally winding down."

"I'm not surprised. It's been an eventful day. Drink up."

Evie finished off her champagne and snuggled down into the covers. "These sheets are so soft," she marveled.

"They're almost as soft as your skin," he said. Evie blushed and Jake grinned, took her glass from her and slid out of bed to take them and what was left of the snacks back to the table. He blew out all the candles and closed the drapes. He double-checked the privacy lock on the door before ducking into the bathroom to brush his teeth.

By the time he got back to the bed, Evie had curled on her side away from him. Soft whiffles of her breath told him that she was fast asleep.

He climbed in, moved over, and curled next to her, his arm across her waist. One of her legs shifted, tangled with his. She gave a deep sigh and settled against him.

Jake stared into the darkness, enjoying the feel of her in his arms. He knew it wouldn't last. She had her life ahead of her, a life that didn't include him. But until then, he'd just enjoy.

CHAPTER EIGHT

"Everything you can find out about Bradley Gaines. Are you taking notes?" Jake paced the sitting area, back and forth, his cell to his ear. He kept his voice low and checked the bedroom every few minutes, but so far Evie hadn't stirred.

Conway's voice came through. "Why would he care about her enough to threaten her? He's been a star for a while now."

He tugged at his damp hair. "Don't know, don't care, just do some digging. I'll work on Evie. I've received two more notes, and trust me. It's not pretty." Seeing the second note, which had been slipped under their door early that morning, had pissed him off. A quick call to the front desk and he learned a kid had dropped the note off, said his mom had seen the show the night before and wanted Evie to get it. The night clerk hadn't seen any reason not to oblige.

But the note was the same as the others, just as threatening in tone. If Evie didn't have a show to do tonight, they'd already be on their way to the next gig in Scottsdale.

His instincts had him on high alert, and there was nothing positive he could do to take out his frustrations. No enemy he could face.

"Okay. I'll get on it. Keep our girl safe, Jake."

"Of course. Call me as soon as you find anything on Gaines." Jake ended the call and flipped his phone against the couch, muttering a string of obscenities. Every nerve in his body was screaming to get them out of there. But a hotel room was safer than a tour bus. At least for now.

A noise behind him had him stiffening.

"You're investigating Brad? Why?"

Jake stilled. Shit. "It's not really an investigation."

"Don't even bother to lie to me." Her voice, usually so warm, was cool. The blade now had an icy edge. "You've been looking for information. I told you my secret shame last night, and now you're suddenly investigating Brad. I call that convenient timing."

He turned. She leaned against the doorway, white sheet wrapped around her, her curls tumbling charmingly around a face set and controlled.

"So, did you seduce me to get the information? Is that how you're going to, how did you put it, 'work on Evie'? If I'd known we were trading orgasms for information, I'd have told you more."

He winced. "You don't know what you're talking about."

A knock on the door. "Room service."

Jake moved to answer the door, watched as Evie moved into the shadows of the bedroom. The waiter came in with a cart, swiftly dealt with the leftovers from the previous night before whipping out a new white tablecloth and setting the table with two plates of food, a carafe of coffee, and a pitcher of orange juice. He left the *USA Today* on one chair.

"Will that be all, sir?"

"Yes. Thank you." Jake signed the bill and the waiter left with the cart. The minute the waiter left, Evie came through the door.

"Well?"

Jake raised an eyebrow. "When you're ready, breakfast is here. We'll talk as we eat."

"First off, once again, I am not a child. I will not be spoken down to, and I will not be treated like some fragile flower who doesn't understand the realities of the world. I lived on the street for almost a year. I can handle it. Whatever it is, I deserve to know." She stalked toward him, dropping the sheet as she walked. "Second of all, this is my life. Mine. I'm the one in charge."

"First off, once again, I've never considered you a child. You're the one who seems to be having an issue about that, not me. Second, I'll be happy to tell you what I know, which isn't a lot, which is only a part of the reason we haven't told you before this. But I'd really appreciate it if you'd get dressed first." He noted, with some satisfaction, a small love bite on the side of her breast.

She crossed her arms. "Really? It bothers you that I'm naked?"

He pinched the bridge of his nose, hoping to stave off a headache. "It bothers me because you're angry, and when you're naked all I want to do is take you back to that bed. But I'm not a huge fan of angry sex, and I don't know you well enough to know what you like. Maybe you get off on angry sex. I don't know." Exasperated, he glared at her. "This is the most ridiculous conversation."

She eyed him. "There's a lot you don't know."

"Which is why I'd prefer it if you would get dressed. That way, we can sit and eat and share information like two adults."

"Oh. So now you're calling me childish? Really?" Abruptly, she tossed her arms in the air and whirled about. Headed for the bedroom.

He followed her, unable to let it go. "I never said you were childish." Jake stopped in the doorway. "I said I wanted to talk like adults, that's all."

"You called me childish by implication," she shot back. She dragged on panties and jeans, pulled on a tee shirt in her favorite sunny yellow and stomped toward him. "Is this dressed enough, or do I have to put on a bra and socks and shoes as well?"

Not knowing what else to do, Jake reached for her, pulled her into the circle of his arms. She stood there, stiff, even as he held her. Rubbed her back. "It's okay. It'll be okay, I promise. It's nothing too terrible. Please don't be mad. I'm just trying to take care of you." He hoped she'd be reasonable. "It's what I do, you know. I protect people."

"I guess." Finally she relaxed. "Hell. What is it?" Her hands came up to his waist. She pulled back a little to look anxiously into his face. "Jake? Please tell me what's going on. Why do I need a bodyguard?"

He sighed. "I told Mike you needed to know. It wasn't my idea to keep you in the dark, but Mike didn't want to worry you."

Her eyebrows rose. "Mike? What does this have to do with Mike?"

Jake steered her to the food. "Let's sit and eat."

She took the cover off her plate. "Scrambled eggs, toast, hash browns, sausage, and fresh fruit. Man. You're a prince, and any other day I'd be all over you kissing your face."

Why had he agreed with Mike and kept her in the dark? That was way stupid. He reached for the carafe of coffee, poured for both of them. "The last few months, since Conway has been sending your demo stuff out, he's been fielding some nasty mail targeting you."

"Nasty like what?" She speared a piece of watermelon.

He kept a careful eye on her. "Like, 'Don't sing or you'll get it. I don't play games, I make promises. Go back into your hole and stop writing songs.' Stupid shit like that. It's why Mike hired me,

Evie. To protect you, figure out who this guy is, and put a stop to it. You don't need this. You certainly don't deserve this."

Her fork clattered out of her hand onto her plate, the remainder of her watermelon untouched. "I knew it." Her eyes were wide, sad.

"Knew what?" He reached across, took her hand. "Talk to me."

"But that's stupid," she argued with herself. "He is so gone from here. Okay, see, ever since we got here, it felt like tweaking the tiger's tail. You know? I told you last night, Vegas is where Brad got his start, years ago, but he's not here now. He's gone. Long gone. Hasn't done a Vegas date in years. None of this makes sense," she declared. "Oh God." She hugged herself, looking a bit shell-shocked.

"You know I'll do everything in my power to keep you safe."

"I know." But she'd started to tremble. "You've received letters here? At the hotel?"

"Yeah. Apparently our guy doesn't do email."

Evie let out a small snort of laughter. "Well, I don't do email, either. And I don't have a cell phone. I'm not plugged in, unless you count the amplifier in my acoustic guitar. I tried to learn songwriting software, but eh." She gave him a lopsided grin. "Guess I'm just an old-fashioned girl."

He stroked her hand. "Maybe that's why he doesn't do email? Because you don't? I suppose you're not on any social media yet, either."

"I don't have anyone to keep in touch with, and I don't have anything to say anyway. No reason for me to twit, or face-whatever." She sniffed and heaved a sigh.

"Can you eat your breakfast now?"

She nodded. "I'm starving. Seriously, thanks for breakfast." She picked up her fork and attacked her scrambled eggs.

"You're welcome." He dug into his own food. "I'm glad you know. It's easier. I need to talk to the local police, and Conway will get back to me with his investigations into Brad."

She frowned and stabbed at her sausage. "Okay. A couple of those phrases you quoted were standard Brad phrases, ones he'd picked up as a teenager trying to be the tough guy. But I owe him for so much. I don't want it to be him. I'm really hoping you're wrong."

"You're hoping I'm wrong, but you're afraid I'm right." Jake reached out and rubbed her shoulder. "I'm hoping I'm wrong, too, then."

"Thank you." She kept her gaze on her food as she talked. "Please keep me in the loop, and keep me near you."

"Don't worry. I'm not letting you out of my sight. So, aside from a visit with the police, do you have anything you want to do today?" He checked the clock. "It's close to one now, and you go on, when? Midnight?"

In a flash, all her tension seemed to disappear. "Ten. I'd love to get some gambling in." Her eyes over-bright, she sent him a saucy grin. "Or shopping. I'd love to go see the Forum Shops, just as soon as I take a nice, hot bath. I've heard about the shops for years, and we didn't get there yesterday. Oh, and can we visit the Paris Hotel? We can get that photo of us in front of the Eiffel Tower, like I mentioned last night. Or was that early this morning?"

He ached at the show she put on, but went with it. "Paris it is, if that's what you really want to do. I'll take care of talking to the police while you're in the bath."

"Ooh, kinda kinky," and waggled her eyebrows, which made him laugh. He didn't understand how her emotions could change so fast, but he did appreciate it. He just hoped he could get away with a phone call, rather than having to go down to the police station.

***

Evie thought she got through breakfast fairly well, but she closed herself in the bathroom with a sigh of relief. She started the bath water and thought about what the morning had revealed.

The first time she woke up it had been to Jake's hands, teasing her. Caressing her. Bringing her to orgasm and slipping into her, taking possession of her body, pleasuring her until she was mindlessly ecstatic. When she tried to wake up, to take control, he'd taken her mouth, kissed her, ruthlessly plunged her into bliss. Sent her straight back to dreamland.

The second time she woke up hadn't been as fun, hearing him on the phone.

She checked the temperature of the running water and turned the hot to medium as she thought about Brad, the threats, and her long-missing songbook. Could that be it? Could he have taken it? But he'd helped her look for it. He'd spent a whole day with her, helping her retrace her steps, asking shopkeepers and bus drivers and teachers about her notebook. Had he just played her, all those years ago?

Hurt sank deep inside. She didn't understand. What had she ever done to him? She *owed* him. He'd kept her safe throughout her childhood. He'd been the one to introduce her to the delights of sex, such as it had been.

Well, they'd been inexperienced then, but he'd been her first love. How could it be otherwise, when he rescued her at such a young age? Of course she'd fallen for him.

What did he think she was going to do? Tell the world how rotten their childhood had been? Not that she was ashamed of her past relationship with him, but it was private, hers alone. If Brad had stuck around, even as a friend, he'd know that about her. But he hadn't.

It was hard to complain about how her life had turned out. If Brad hadn't left her, she'd never have run away. But because Brad *had* left, and she *had* run away, first Mike and then Jake had come into her life. And while watching Mike die had been so hard, being with Jake was surprisingly, wonderfully, easy. Except when he was being a stubborn, stuffy, irritatingly protective male, which really went without saying.

She added bubbles to the bathwater and stripped then climbed in. The heat sank into her bones and she relaxed, glad to soak after their adventurous night. She hadn't had the most exciting sex life, though she knew what she liked. She'd learned early on to be picky about sleeping partners. Thanks again to Brad.

Being with Jake was like, oh, hitting the jackpot. He was sexy, confident, primitive, totally an alpha male with a stuffy yet warm side to him. It must all stem from having sisters. How could she not be bowled over by his attentions?

But Evie was a realist down to her DNA. She had a long, hard climb ahead of her in order to get to the top. She had a good head for business, though no patience for school. Once she started making a living at what she loved to do, then the rest would fall into place. Until then, relationships were temporary. Made for the short term, to satisfy the needs of friendship and sex.

"Temporary" had always been her mantra, and while she'd been learning the songwriting business with Mike, and then taking care of him, she'd barely had time for even temporary relationships. More like friends with benefits, on those few occasions she got shooed out of the house by Mike.

It had worked for a long time. There was absolutely no reason to change her ways at this point. So why did the thought of a temporary relationship with Jake make her heart sink?

Nerves, she decided, and she sank below the water line to get her hair wet. She came up, sputtering. Only nerves.

"Hey in there. Are you almost done?" *Jake.*

She couldn't stop herself from grinning. "Uh, no. I've barely been in here five minutes." She reached for the shampoo and washed her hair.

"The faster you're out of there, the faster you can go and gamble and then do some shopping. If I'm going shopping, I don't want it to be forever before we leave here," he added.

"Okay, okay. I'm just washing my hair, and then soaping up my body. All over. Slowly," she added, picking up the bar of soap and suiting her actions to the words.

Silence from the other side of the door.

"Jake? You there?"

He cleared his throat. "Yeah. Uh. Just getting the mental picture clear in my mind. How high is the water?"

"Ha ha, you're funny. I'll be out in a few minutes, I swear. Okay, maybe more like ten minutes. But I don't have to get all fussy, so just let me bathe. Oh, and could you call the front desk about my red dress? It really does need a cleaning," she added and bit her thumbnail.

"You bet. You've got ten minutes before I knock down the door. Enjoy your bath."

"Ooh, threats," she muttered, still grinning. Yeah. Who would have thought she'd be on her first tour and get a knockout lover to boot?

Life was just full of mysteries.

She rushed through her bath, rinsing her hair and body with the shower as the bathwater drained away. She took the time to slick on some of her favorite lotion and used the hair dryer, a brush, and curl tamer to bring some sense of order to the wild thing that was her mop of curls.

Once done, she grabbed a dry towel, wrapped herself in it, and opened the bathroom door.

Jake was hunched over his computer. "Oh good, you're out." He didn't look up.

"I am. The water was lovely." She picked through her underwear, found a bright blue thong and slipped it on. Put on the matching demi-bra. Since today was their last day in Vegas, she'd wear her sundress. White with wide straps, it had a huge abstract floral pattern. White flats, and she was ready.

"Done," she said, and turned to check out Jake.

He was still fixated on his computer. And he was wearing a suit. Man, that was totally stuffy. And he looked so hot. Stuffy and hot, and she needed her head examined.

"I think there might be a law against wearing a suit in Las Vegas, Mr. Stuffy." He didn't answer. Frowning, she sauntered over to him, ran her hand through his hair. "Hello, it's me. I'm ready. Knock knock. Hello Jake, are you there?" Exasperated, she put her hands on her hips. "Seriously? What is wrong with you?"

He finally looked up at her and his eyes weren't quite in focus. "I'm sorry. I just got some news. I think I'm in shock," he added.

"What?" Concerned, she sat next to him. "What's wrong? Is there anything I can do to help? Anything at all?"

He gave a helpless little shrug. "It's Joy. Joy and Thorne. Dear God."

Alarmed, Evie slugged him. "Damn you. What's *wrong*?"

"She's pregnant," he said. "With twins. She's the baby, and she's going to have babies. I'm definitely in shock," he added, and looked hurt when Evie burst into the giggles.

"You're such a nut," she said, and full of affection for him, she kissed his cheek. "Come on. We'll go get baby clothes. If she knows she's having twins, then she must be over three months, right? I thought she was using the bathroom rather frequently at my house."

She stood, tugged at his hand. "Close up your computer and come on. We need to gamble, shop for me, and shop for the babies."

"Babies," he said, still dazed. He stood and followed her. "What am I going to do? They're so small, babies. I've never had to watch out for anything that small, that fragile."

She found her purse where she'd put it in the closet, slung it over her shoulder. "I find that hard to believe. You mean none of your other sisters have kids?"

"That's not the point. Joy's the youngest. She's the baby. She's always been the baby."

She took his hand as they walked the corridor to the elevator. "So the baby is all grown up. What are you going to do, now that your chicks have flown the nest for real?"

They stopped in front of the elevator. Jake's gaze settled on her face, his eyes finally focusing, and he smiled. Wolfishly. "Start living my own life," he said.

Evie, not certain what that gleam in his eye meant, squeezed his hand, and when the elevator opened, she stepped into it. They were the only passengers. She pressed the button for the ground floor and the doors closed silently.

Just as silently, Jake turned to her, framed her face with his hands, bent and kissed her. "Good afternoon, my lovely and talented companion. I'm going to be an uncle. Again. Twice in one go. Isn't that amazing?"

She laughed and kissed him back. Hugged him hard. "You are so damned cute. I knew you had a heart of mush under the stuffy suit and protective nonsense you flaunt."

He grinned, flicked the tip of her nose. "If you think I've been overprotective of you, you should really talk to my sisters. By the way, did you bring your sunglasses with you? Did you put on sunscreen?"

Evie just laughed at him.

She wasn't laughing ten minutes later. Jake had stopped in the hotel's convenience store and bought her a pair of sunglasses and sunscreen; then he proceeded to spread the sunscreen on her upper back, her chest, and her arms while they stood in the lobby.

Evie rolled her eyes. "Really, Jake. I can do it myself."

"You could. But then I couldn't have my hands all over you with every man in the lobby jealous of me." He pressed a kiss on her lips, dotted her forehead and cheekbones with sunscreen. "Rub that in."

Evie looked around while smoothing on the lotion. "Well, all the women want to be me, so there." Despite her protests, having him spread sunscreen on her was awfully cute. Except… "If I'd made a big stink about it, you'd have let me do it myself, right?"

He pretended to be offended. "Of course. Believe it or not, I'm not a control freak. I'm just careful. Plus I like touching you, and doing it in public is fun." He winked and put the cap on the sunscreen. "Can you fit this in your purse?"

She sighed. "I can. Let's go down the strip and try a new casino. I feel I'll be luckier in an unfamiliar place."

He tucked her hand through his arm. "I thought the Four Parrots was pretty lucky so far, but whatever you say."

The heat hit them the minute they stepped outside. "Vegas in the summertime is so much fun," Jake muttered.

"You're the one wearing the suit," she pointed out. "You could have worn vacation clothes."

He gestured to a man just heading into the hotel. "Like him, with plaid shorts, flip flops, and a tank top? I'd rather die. Let's take a taxi to Caesar's Palace. That way you can gamble and shop all in the same place."

"Brilliant."

The ride was short, and when they got there the casino was noisy and humming with life. "Did you bring your cash?"

"Yep. The money I won yesterday." She patted her purse. "I'm so ready."

"Do yourself a favor. Only gamble with twenty of it, so you're gambling with the house's money."

"Stuffy, yet practical advice. Excellent. I'm glad you're here," and she squeezed his arm as they made their way to the slot machines. "Ooh, looky, there's a *Twilight* quarter machine. Let's do that one." She steered him to a machine and patted the stool next to hers. "Come on."

"Seriously?"

She beamed. "Yep. See? If you get one werewolf, one human, and one vampire, you win. And if you get the big three, a Jacob, a Bella, and an Edward, you win really big." She fed in her twenty and rubbed her hands in anticipation. "I am so going to win big."

For the next hour, Jake watched as Evie's fortunes rose and fell with each tap of the button. She looked so genuinely delighted with the game and their surroundings that he just relaxed and enjoyed her. Pushed the problem of her stalker to the back of his mind. Nothing he could do right now, anyway, except worry.

Instead, he watched her play. Learned how she pouted as the number of quarters she had left dwindled down to a dozen before hitting a string of small wins. She twitched on the seat with every roll of the machine, and bounced when she won.

He got lost in her throaty laugh, the sparkle in her eyes whenever they talked. So he did his best to keep her laughing with his comments about werewolves and vampires.

As they walked away from the slots and toward the shopping area, Evie chattering excitedly about the money she'd won, Jake abruptly realized he'd spent more than an hour watching a woman play a slot machine. Not only that, but he'd been entranced with her. Besotted. Befuddled. Bewitched and every other be-word he could think of.

Holy hell. He was dangerously close to falling in love.

CHAPTER NINE

They window shopped at the high-end stores in the casino. Evie found some cute little baby clothes, which Jake talked her out of buying. She learned that he liked jewelry stores, didn't much care for clothing stores except the men's suit section, and didn't read much popular literature.

But they both liked a temporary art installation in one corner of the shopping area. The paintings were either angry abstracts or romance-drenched landscapes. Their conversation about art carried through their very late lunch at Gordon Ramsay Pub and Grill. By the time they returned to their hotel via taxi, it was past six in the evening.

"Man, the food was totally awesome." Evie yawned as she toed off her shoes. She rubbed her tummy. "All I want to do is take a nap now. Think you can join me?"

"I'm glad you had a good time. Settle in. I've got some work to do." Jake moved to the desk and retrieved his laptop from the top drawer, where he'd stashed it earlier, since the safe was too small. "When do you want me to wake you up?"

She pouted. She'd really wanted to just snuggle for a bit. "Before eight. I need to warm up, take a shower, you know." She waved vaguely and he laughed.

"I promise I'll wake you before eight. Nap well."

Evie stripped off her dress and the bra, hung both on a hanger in the closet. She got into bed exhausted, but it was nothing a nap wouldn't cure. She pondered the day, especially the part that neither of them had mentioned once.

They had talked to the cops, who took the letters into custody. They promised to get in touch with the San Diego PD. Everyone seemed to believe that the possibility of finding fingerprints, much less actually identifying the person who sent them, were just about zero.

No one had died. Nor had the threats truly escalated. They were annoying, yes, and maybe a bit sinister, but until something big happened, there wasn't much anyone could do. Evie sighed. She'd be better off putting all this out of her head, and concentrating on her music, and tonight's performance.

But the funny thing was, once they left the police department, nothing more was said about it. In the hours they'd spent together, neither one of them had brought up the stalker or the fact that it might just be her first love.

And Jake. What was she going to do about Jake? She'd never really had a buddy before, someone to shop with and laugh with and eat a frivolous lunch with. The fact that he'd done all those things, plus watched her play a slot machine, and best of all was a fabulous lover, just totally blew her mind. He'd cooled since they got back tonight, but seriously, was she going to complain? Uh, no. She'd never lived in someone's pocket before, so being with him every hour of the day was different. Unusual. She rather thought he wasn't used to it, either.

Bossy? Yes. Possessive? Decidedly. Revved her engines? Abso-fucking-lutely. So what the hell was she going to do with him? She rolled over, thumped a pillow, and shut her eyes. The hushing white noise of the air conditioner and Jake's tapping of his keyboard blended together to create a soft river of sound amongst the silence. Up so high they didn't hear traffic. As they were at the end of the hallway, they rarely heard other people.

She let her mind drift. The melody she'd been working on came back to her. Energy poured through her and she pushed off the covers, went to the dresser for a tee shirt and a pair of yoga pants and dressed. Work would clear her mind faster than pretending to rest.

"Jake?"

"Hm?"

"Call for coffee, please? I've got work to do. Hope I won't disturb you," she added, and settled on the couch with her guitar and a pad of paper.

"What about your nap?"

She smiled and shrugged. He looked so put out because she wasn't napping. "When the muse hits, I gotta go with it. And she's hitting something hard right now, so excuse me." Evie spent the next few minutes tuning the instrument. Done, she put the electronic tuner aside and finger-picked the melody she'd noodled with on the trip out. She got lost in the notes. Coffee appeared at her elbow and she sucked some in before diving back into the melody. Finally, the words came.

Looking for a long time/Not knowing what or why/I drifted and I waited/Time seemed to pass me by/But then my world died and/Life took a different turn—and home is where I found you.

Evie allowed herself to drown in the words, in the tune. Played with both, scratching out and rewriting the lyrics, and noodling with the melody by changing it up, going fast here, slow there.

Home isn't quite a place and/I'd never known before/That home didn't necessarily/Have windows or a door/But now when I think of you/Home's what comes to mind—

Happiness beat through her. This is what she lived for, what she loved to do. How many people could say they loved what they did for a living? Elated, she read the lyrics she'd written, frowned. Scratched out a few more words, and started over again, fitting melody to the words.

She hadn't had this much fun writing songs since before Mike had gotten sick. Lyrics had always come easy, but it was hard to memorize the notes when you didn't know what the heck the notes were.

Brad had never bothered to teach her the guitar, and he'd always kept it in his room. His brother Ted had bought it for him, and it was Brad's most prized possession. He was forever warning her to never touch it, so she never had.

But she'd watched him like a hawk and asked him to name the chords he played so she could note them down. He probably hadn't realized she had been trying to memorize the finger positioning on the strings. He'd been so caught up in his dreams that he'd stopped seeing her.

Evie caught sight of Jake's head, bent to his computer, and her heart thumped. Hard. Jake wouldn't have been so selfish. It was weird, having him there. Since Brad had left, she never made music with someone else around. Even with Mike, she'd gone into a different room to compose. He would hear her of course, but he couldn't see her, and he never commented on her work while it was in progress. He always waited until she finished composing and played the song for him before he mentioned it.

This was new, this sharing her music so intimately. She hadn't even shared lyrics with Brad until she was done. But Jake didn't play music or speak the language, so creating in front of him felt deeply personal. Like being naked, only times a hundred. She sighed.

Her thoughts drifted to her notebook, the one that had gone missing so long ago. So much time had passed that there was no way she could ever re-create it. She wasn't eleven, twelve, thirteen anymore and hadn't been for a long time. Her life had been so tumbled in the year she spent on the streets that anything she'd written prior to that time would seem childish to her now.

But she would give anything to have it again. A record of her past. A new melody wove itself through her mind and she set her coffee down, picked up her guitar. This song, now, was more of a patter song, lots of words and little musical flourish. Just a steady beat. But what did all the words say? Too many ran through her mind. Her gaze kept straying to Jake. Her mind filled with him.

She abandoned the guitar and picked up her notebook. Words flowed onto the page without hesitation. Protector. Stuffy. Handsome as sin. Funny. Amazing lover. Dark hair and deep blue eyes. She kept the pen moving, the words coming, and her spirit stretched and soared as she worked.

***

After setting the coffee near Evie, Jake went back to the desk where he kept his focus on his computer, despite his curiosity to watch her at work. He opened the email from Conway, read a few lines, and cursed softly. There'd been a break-in attempt at Evie's house, but the new alarm system Jake had urged Conway to install had stood up to the task and frightened the burglars away. The cops didn't have anything to go on.

The next bit of the message was an eye-opener, though. Bradley Gaines was in deep trouble. Tax evasion, plus domestic assault and battery. According to Conway, his last album had been a bust, too, out a week and hadn't moved more than ten thousand units.

Not good for a guy who'd had five number-one hits in a row. Jake steepled his fingers as he pondered this latest news. Normally he wouldn't care some rocker's sales or musical quality. But since Brad and Evie had a connection, and Evie was on the rise, Brad could very well be feeling threatened. But why?

There had to be more, somewhere. Maybe if Brad and Evie met face to face, all the intrigue would stop. Of course, Brad was Evie's first love. She might want to reunite with him. Work with him, maybe. Collaborate on songs, cozy up in a recording studio, be seen around town. Maybe even go to the Grammys together.

Jake pinched the bridge of his nose. God, he hated feeling like this. Jealousy twisted his gut and for what reason? None. He pushed back from the desk.

Evie's head came up and her smile lit up her whole face. "You okay? I'm not bugging you?"

Why the hell was she so happy? "I'm fine. Need to hit the gym. I'd run outside, but I don't want to die from heatstroke," he added. "You don't mind?"

"Nah. I'm fine. You are coming to the show tonight, right?"

He sent her a swift smile. "I'll be here to escort you down." He headed to the bedroom, went to the dresser, found his gym clothes. He hung up his suit jacket, stripped out of his shirt and hung that and his pants up, too. He dressed in his shorts, kept on his white tee shirt, and changed his shoes. He didn't want to leave her, but man. He needed some serious exercise to shake him loose, get his mind back in the game. Get his mind off her.

He came back into the main room. "I'll be gone about an hour."

"I'm sure I'll find something to do," she said wryly.

She looked so pretty there, with her guitar in her lap. He pocketed his room key and his phone. He gave in to temptation, and went to her side, tilted her head up.

"Think of me," he ordered, and kissed her, a swift, hard kiss that brought a slight daze to her eyes when they parted, Jake noted. He kissed her again. "That should hold me." He tousled her hair before heading out the door.

As he did his five miles on the treadmill, he focused in on Evie. Again. What the hell made her so special? Aside from the total sweetness of her. And her tendency to just blurt out whatever she thought, which was pretty funny.

"Plus, hello. Sexy woman," he muttered.

The redhead next to him turned and grinned. "Thanks. It's been a while since anyone's said that to me. I gotta say, you're pretty sexy, too," she said giving him the up and down.

Jake shot her a dubious look as he ran. "Sorry. I was thinking out loud." He stepped up his speed and ignored the woman's disappointment. She looked to be in her fifties and was in great shape, but she didn't sparkle like Evie.

Nobody sparkled like Evie. What *didn't* make her special?

Though being in this predicament wasn't his fault. He could blame Mike for setting them up. His sisters set him up all the time, but somehow, he'd always managed to catch wind of it early. Keep his guard firmly in place. Mike hadn't given off that matchmaking vibe when he talked about Evie. He had made her sound like a precious, adorable, intelligent, *nine*-year-old.

Of course, he could always blame the moonlit beach. He *knew* better, damn it. He did. Hadn't he proposed to Cop Girl on a moonlit beach? He hadn't even planned it. The question just sort of spilled out. What a disaster that marriage had been. Since the divorce, he'd kept women at arms' length, rarely keeping a relationship going for more than a couple of months before he slipped away.

"No harm, no foul. Bull." He thumped the bar in front of him for emphasis.

"I don't know, buddy. That ball looked like a foul to me. Maybe they'll replay it."

Jake checked out the baseball game playing on the screen in front of them and glanced at the runner on his other side. A buff man in his mid-thirties wearing skin-tight shorts gave him the once-over and winked appreciatively.

Jake coughed. "Ah. The game is on. Sorry. Talking to myself."

He turned away and grabbed the water bottle he'd bought at the entrance to the gym. Guzzled it as he ran. What was wrong with the people in this gym, anyway? You don't talk to strangers in a gym. Having to sweat next to strangers was bad enough. He much preferred to run in Balboa Park, but baby, he was a long way from doing that.

Why, by all that was holy, did he think he'd be any better at a relationship now? With someone over a decade younger, no less? He was just asking to be cheated on again. Women like Evie, just entering a long sexual prime, must need a lot of male companionship. Of course she'd find someone who wasn't *stuffy* to hang around. Technically, the deal they'd agreed on tendered their relationship over when they reached San Diego. If he pursued it further with her, assuming she'd be agreeable, it would be the same as begging her to cheat on him. Basically cutting off his balls so she could put them in her purse.

"My balls, her purse," he muttered, and wiped the sweat out of his eyes.

The woman next to him laughed. "Oh honey, you've got it bad," she said, chortling.

Jake slapped the big red 'OFF' button and glared at the woman. "What?"

"You're in love, aren't you?" The redhead wiped the sweat from her face with a pale blue towel. "I can tell. You're in love, and you're none too happy about it."

The guy on his other side stepped off his treadmill and joined them. "I know, right? With his balls in her purse, he's a goner."

"I'm not in love, and my balls are right where they should be." He didn't need to parade personal feelings around strangers. "For Pete's sake." He grabbed the towel, wiped his head, and tried not to listen to the two of them.

"You know, he probably brought her here for some fun and games. And now he found how serious he really is about her, and he's scared to death," Redhead said to Tight Shorts, who nodded his agreement.

Tight Shorts crossed his arms and stood hipshot as he eyed Jake again. "Oh yes. From here, they'll part forever because he's too chicken to start over. Too scared to live the life he's always wanted," Tight Shorts said with a sigh. He put a friendly arm around Redhead and they strolled on. "Hey doll, do you watch The Soap Network? I'm just catching up with Luke and Laura's wedding on *General Hospital* reruns."

"Oh honey, let me tell you, I watched it the first time around on network TV, and it just about wrecked me for a normal relationship. Hey, did you hear about this hot new singer? Her name is Evie something. Want to go with me to tonight's show? I've got tix. Here in the hotel, even."

Jake stared after the two as they headed off to the free weights, chatting like they were old friends. What had just happened here? And wait, they were talking about Evie's show? He had to tell her that.

There was one good thing about this trip, he mused. Yes, they were leaving Las Vegas in the morning, but their journey wasn't over. He had time to sort this all out.

Jake tossed the damp towel into the bin, chugged the rest of his water, and dropped the bottle in the recycle bin before pushing out of the gym. His head didn't feel any clearer, but his body hummed from the exercise. Better than a kick in the head any day.

One thing was certain, he vowed as he headed toward the elevators. Whatever happened, his balls weren't going to end up in any woman's purse. He needed to make sure Evie knew where the line was drawn, and he wasn't talking about her collarbone this time.

If he wanted to keep sleeping with her, then she needed to know the score. They both needed to know the score, he amended wryly.

"Excuse me, Mr. Wells?" It was the same front desk manager.

Jake stopped, dreading the news. "Yes?"

"You asked me to hold messages, but I thought these were important and I saw that you'd checked into the gym, so." The young man handed over a fistful of pink message slips.

Jake shuffled through them quickly and smiled. "Thank you. Tell Mr. Beyers that we'll meet him in an hour in the club."

"I will do so. Thank you, sir."

Jake waited for the elevator and grinned, his personal issues for the moment pushed aside. Hot damn, Evie was a media darling. He couldn't wait to tell her.

CHAPTER TEN

Evie lifted one leg up out of the bathwater and soaped it, pretending to be the heroine in her favorite historical novel, where hot baths were rare except for the very wealthy. Soon the hero would come in, she mused, picturing Jake standing in the doorway with a billowy white shirt open to his navel, wearing skin-tight breeches and riding boots, his eyes dark with anger and lust.

She rinsed her leg and soaped the other one. The hero, having interrupted the heroine during her bath, would be overcome by her bare, glistening flesh. He'd drag her out of the water, dripping wet, and kiss her senseless. All over.

After rinsing her other leg, she lay back in the bathwater and swooshed her head around, getting her hair wet. Sitting up again, she shampooed and rinsed. As before, she let the bathwater out and turned the shower on for a final warm rinse.

The bathroom door burst open and the shower curtain swept aside. Evie stared at Jake and her heart pounded. He wasn't wearing a billowy white shirt, but she'd take him. "Hi." She cursed her breathlessness, praying he wouldn't notice.

"Hi." He gave her an appreciative glance, pulled his shirt off over his head, and shucked his shorts. "Move over, I'm coming in. We've got an appointment in a little under an hour."

"An appointment?" She moved aside to give him the spray. The workout must have done him some good, for Jake buzzed with energy. He gave her a smacking kiss on the cheek.

"Plus, the band wants to meet. The club manager wants to talk to all of you about a return engagement, and you've got an interview set up with the *Las Vegas Weekly*. Oh, and you're trending on Twitter."

Evie watched as he soaped up his hard body, barely tracking his words. "Okay. Whatever 'trending on Twitter' means." Even though they'd spent the night together, the remnants of her fantasy made her shy. And lusty.

"So go. Get dressed. We need to be downstairs as soon as possible."

"What? Why?" Puzzled, she lifted her gaze to meet his. She reached out and smoothed the water rolling off his shoulders. "I'd much rather just hop back into bed with you," she confessed.

Jake blew out a breath. "Whoo boy. Hold that thought, sweetheart. You've got meetings. An interview, then a show. Go get dressed," he said, grinning. "It's the beginning of the big time, baby."

"Oh. Oh!" She stepped out of the tub and grabbed a towel, dried her hair and body as fast as possible. "I can do this, I can do this," she chanted as she left the bathroom, leaving the door open wide.

The next ten minutes were a scramble as both of them dressed. Jake wore a dark suit. Evie chose bright yellow short overalls, a pink tee shirt, and pink Converse Hi-tops. Evie checked him out and groaned.

"I look like a kid."

"You're fine."

"But you look so sophisticated, and I look like poor white trash. Oh God, my hair."

"You look fresh and sweet and when they hear you tonight, you will blow them away. Stop worrying." He tightened the knot on his tie and settled his jacket. "I'll get your dresses. May as well take them down, too. What about your makeup bag?"

"I'll get it."

She escaped to the bathroom, grateful that most of the steam had gone. Clutching the marble counter, she stared at her reflection. "I can do this. No one can make me feel inferior without my consent. I own my voice. I own my talent. I am not ashamed of my journey." She caught her breath. "Oh Mike. I so wish you were here."

"Evie? Let's move."

Evie moved.

***

The entrance to the club was unlocked, and when Evie and Jake entered, they saw the rest of the band gathered at a table toward the front. The club manager hadn't yet shown.

"Hey, guys."

Jake cleared his throat. "I'll just put your stuff in the dressing room."

"What there is of it," said Bear. Jimmy chuckled nervously. Reid shifted in his chair.

Evie watched Jake find his way backstage and settled across from Bear. "So what's the buzz?"

"A couple things," Bear said. "First, you sounded real good last night, Evie. I liked the order of things, and wanted to know if you had any changes in mind."

"I thought it went well. I'm fine with leaving it the way it is. What else?"

The three of them shared glances.

Evie's gut clenched. "Just tell me. I'm a big girl."

"And you're playing on the edge of the big time now," Bear said heavily. "There's a rumor going around on Twitter about you."

Her heart thumped. "Uh, okay. Jake said something to that effect but he didn't say what it was about." She searched the somber faces opposite her. "What is it?"

Bear reached across the table, took her hand into his big paw. "There's been some talk about you."

She immediately thought of the night she and Jake had spent, and blushed. "Really? But that's private."

Jake crossed the stage, heading toward them. She turned to him in mute appeal. Jake frowned. "Bear?" He moved to stand behind her, his hand on her shoulder. "What's going on?"

Bear's gaze went from one face to the other, and he smiled, shook his head. "I'm not asking about your personal life, Evie. He looks like a good one, so if he's warming your bed there's nothing wrong with it."

She cursed the heat in her cheeks. "Then what? Just say it."

"Someone's saying, well, your songs, well, that you didn't write 'em. We know it's not true, but we don't know how to sway public opinion." Bear shook his shaggy head.

"Wait. What?" Evie looked from one member of the band to another. "Someone's saying what?"

Reid drummed his fingers on the table. "Can't prove you wrote 'em, even though you did. I remember you working on these songs, just after we heard about Mike getting sick."

"It was your way of coping, we all knew that," added Jimmy. "I helped you a bit once, with the chording, on Soul Savior. Remember?"

"Someone saw the show last night, and started the ruckus this morning. I'm sorry, Evie," Bear added. "It sucks, but I don't know what to do."

Jake's hand tightened on Evie's shoulder. He came around and sat next to her. "I told you about the stalker, Bear."

"That was kid stuff," Bear said. "Paper. They hadn't taken it to the Internet."

"It did occur to me that he could, but there was no way I could stop him from going there." Jake's voice was clipped and hard.

Bear shrugged and nodded. "If it isn't the same guy, then it's odd."

"Oh damn." Evie dropped her head in her hands. "Okay, spill it. Tell me everything."

Bear grimaced. "Johnny M, the Beast of Social Media, has been teasing bits of an interview on Twitter. He hasn't yet tweeted his source."

Evie closed her eyes. Even though she wasn't big on the computer stuff, or social media, she had heard of Johnny M. He was kind of like a more-twisted Perez Hilton, which said a lot about the type of story he liked to run.

"But it started before that, in a good way," Reid said. "After the shows last night, I saw several tweets about you and the club. All positive. They got picked up and had a good run. This morning, there was even a brief bit in one of the freebie papers the hotel puts out, calling you a rising star."

"Then the Beast hit Twitter."

Evie blew out a breath. "Tell me what they're saying."

Bear pulled out a paper from his pocket. "I had to write them down. Hope you don't mind." He passed it over. "You should just read."

#EvieM is @clubblack. #notforreal #suchafake #dontgo

#EvieM is a #plagiarist says #realbigstar

Don't fall for #EvieM @clubblack #plagiarist #hack #breakyourheart

@JohnnyMBeast has the #scoop on #EvieM #bethere

The "at" symbols and hashtags looked strange. She knew about Twitter, of course, who didn't? But not having a phone or any sort of computer meant she never really needed to think about it before.

"What—I don't understand. How can they think I didn't write the songs? I've got my notebooks. Oh my God." Evie groped for Jake's hand, clutched it tight as awareness dawned. "I have every notebook I've ever written in, except for one." She swallowed and gazed at each of her bandmates. "I lost that notebook when I was fifteen. If people are saying my songs are similar to someone else's, maybe that's because someone used that notebook."

Jake crouched down beside her. "You think it's Brad."

She flinched at his statement. "I don't want to think." Evie handed the paper back to Bear. "They are lies. You know that, right?"

He nodded. "Course we know. I'm awfully sorry, sweetheart."

Jake took Evie's hand in his. "This may get worse before it gets better. Depending on who we're dealing with, there may be a lawsuit."

The numbness that had gripped Evie slowly gave way to anger. "If there is, we'll survive it. At least we can still sing for our supper."

"For now," Jimmy said, his eyes troubled. "I've got two kids. If we lose gigs, then I'll need to look for work with another band. You understand, right, Evie?"

She did understand. She reached for his hand, squeezed it. "Absolutely. We all have to do what's best for our lives. I just ask you to hang in there for this tour, since it's so short. I don't know if Conway's booked anything else yet. Just give it some time. Can you do that?"

Bear spoke. "We can do that. You know we love you, Evie. You've been around for so long. Mike told us to watch out for you, so we will. We'll have your back. Well, Reid and I will, anyway."

"Hey." Jimmy punched Bear on the shoulder. "I had to say it."

"Yeah. You did." Evie rubbed her eyes, grateful she hadn't yet put on her stage makeup. "What's next?"

"Mr. Beyers, the club manager, should be here any minute," Jake said. He glanced at his phone.

"I don't know whether to be excited that he wants to talk to us, or worried." Evie leaned against Jake.

He put an arm around her. "It'll be fine. Remember, all publicity is good publicity. And when this is put to rest and you come out of it looking like the star that you are, you'll get the sympathy vote, too."

"Not sure the sympathy vote is what we're really after," Reid said. "This sucks, Evie. I'm so sorry."

"Well, there they are," boomed a voice from the back of the audience. Evie and Jake turned to look. Jake stood.

"Mr. Beyers. Let me get you a chair."

"No need, no need." The big man came toward them, surprisingly light on his feet. With his dyed hair and smooth face, it was impossible to guess his age. "Just wanted to let you folks know that we're sold out at our ten o'clock. We never sell that show out, so I have to think it's all due to you. Want to talk to you about a return engagement, say maybe in October."

The band exchanged glances, but it was Jake that spoke up. "You can talk to their manager, Conway Davis. I'm pretty sure you have his number, but if you need it again I can get it to you."

Beyers grinned. "I've got it. Just wanted to get a head start, get my claim in, before other clubs snap you up. I had my publicity team spark you last night after the first show, but Twitter really took off. And now with those rumors, it's all good."

"They aren't true, by the way," Bear said. "The rumors."

"Don't care. I mean, it's good to know, but whatever gets asses in the seats, you know? By the way, my midnight talent canceled. Will you stay and do that show, too?"

Evie looked at Bear, who winked. "Oh, I don't know," she began. "It's our last night in Vegas, and I so wanted to go out on the town."

"I'll double your rate."

"For both shows tonight." Evie arched an eyebrow, and the manager laughed.

"Okay. For both shows. I can handle it because we're sold out." He stuck his hand out, and Evie shook it. "Thank you. This is the best we've done all year. Being all the way out at the far end of the Strip, we don't see much action," he said. "Not that I'm complaining." He rubbed his hands together. "I'd better get the word out that you're playing the second show. Oh, and there's a reporter here to see you."

"We've been expecting him, so yeah, go ahead and send him in."

"Her, actually," Beyers said. "Lana Kirkland. Bit of a shark. She's local, but has aspirations, if you get my drift. I'll tell her you'll see her. By the way, any of you need anything? Water, iced tea, hot tea, coffee, anything?"

"A round of bottled water would be great." Bear stood up. "I'll help you with that." The two men went to the bar.

Evie held her stomach, praying she wouldn't be sick. "God, I'm nervous."

"You'll be fine. There's nothing to worry about." Jake stroked her back.

"Why do you think they want an interview? It's because of the rumor, isn't it?"

"We've got your back, Evie." Bear had returned, setting cold bottles of water on the table. "We stay unified."

"Remember, it's up to you as to how much you tell her. She's not your best friend, but she's not your enemy, either. How you treat her will go into her column, you can bet on that," Jake said. He stood, pulled a face. "I'll just be over there, acting like a bodyguard. Within your eyesight."

Evie considered him. "We could always say you're a new member of the band."

"Maraca player?"

Evie giggled. "I guess not. And if she asks who you are?"

"You can look at her, surprised, and say, 'what man standing where?' You got this, Evie."

His confidence in her made her sit a little taller. "Of course I do. Piece of cake."

Bear caught her eye. "That reporter's coming. Be careful."

"Got it."

Reid sighed heavily. "I wish I'd asked for iced tea," he said mournfully.

Evie and Jimmy cracked up.

Bear stood. "Good evening, Ms. Kirkland."

Evie eyed her. Sleek, expensive, and closer to thirty than twenty. A delicate perfume drifted in the air. Her honey-brown hair was pulled back into a thick ponytail that curled at the end. Her business suit was a pale green and she had paired a shocking pink top with it. Shrewd eyes hid behind black-rimmed glasses.

"Good evening." The voice was smooth. Accentless. "I take it you're the band?"

"Evie and the Gang. Please, have a seat. Let me introduce you to everyone." Bear made the introductions and pulled out a chair for her next to him.

Evie smiled. This woman may look like a barracuda, but there was no sense in being hostile. Yet.

"So, Evie. I'm hearing some amazing things about you."

"Thank you. I do hope you're planning on seeing the show tonight, so you can judge for yourself. Which paper do you work for?" She kept her eyes wide on the other woman.

"The *Las Vegas Weekly*. Plus I do daily blog posts for them."

Evie clasped her hands together. "Very cool. I know nothing about blogs. I have to confess, I'm not plugged into the Internet at all."

The other woman instantly put on a sympathetic face. "You've had a hard time of it, I understand."

Surprised, Evie laughed. "Where did you hear that?"

"Oh, well." She looked down at a small notebook. "I understand you lived with Mike Harper. That you organized his wake. May I record this?" Lana dug in her purse and put a small digital recorder on the table between them.

"Of course."

"So. Mike Harper?"

"He was a wonderful man. He took me in when I needed help, and we were roommates for just over ten years. I owe him more than I could possibly repay." Evie took a sip of her water.

"You organized his wake, correct?" she repeated.

"He left me detailed instructions, so it was pretty straightforward. Yes, I did organize it. It was a wonderful event." Evie's gaze strayed to Jake and she smiled.

He smiled back. Evie caught her breath and switched her gaze to the reporter, who looked intrigued.

"Everyone likes stories of beginnings, and this is your first club date. How did it come about?"

"Mike was my mentor, my teacher. I learned to play and sing with these guys, friends of his in the business," and she gestured to the band. "We'd play on the beach every now and then, just informally. Mike's manager happened to drop by one afternoon and heard us. The rest is kind of history."

"So Mike really manipulated your life," Lana mused.

Evie shook her head dismissively. "No. Not manipulated. We were friends."

"Not lovers?" Lana's tone could only be called arch.

Evie laughed. "No. He'd be horrified if you even suggested it to him. He was more like a parent to me than anything. Very strict."

"How old were you when you two moved in together?"

The questions were beginning to get on her nerves. "We became *roommates*"—Evie stressed the word—"when I was just sixteen."

"Why?"

Evie smiled. "I'd rather not answer that question in detail. But in general, I needed a place to live."

"Do you have any idea of who is spreading rumors about you?"

"The ones that The Beast is circulating?" she shrugged. "Don't know. Don't really care, either. They're not true. The two songs I wrote, that I sang last night, were done a couple of years ago."

Lana smiled, her eyes sharpened. "I was told you'd deny it."

"Really? Who told you that? Because the people in this room were a part of my life when I wrote those songs. Which are in a dated notebook, along with about a hundred other songs, most of which will never see the light of day."

"So his information is accurate. You do write down your songs in a notebook. Spiral bound, college ruled, is that right?"

Despite her rising nausea, Evie just raised an eyebrow. "I'm sorry. Who did you say was accurate in his information?"

Lana changed the subject with a thin-lipped smile. "So where does Evie and the Gang go from here?"

Bear spoke up. "Scottsdale next, then Los Angeles. But we'll be back here. We like the Four Parrots."

"You do?" She seemed astonished at his announcement.

Evie laughed. "I even won a whole fifty dollars on a slot machine here," she said. "This is my first trip out of California."

Lana clucked her tongue. "You poor thing."

Evie just smiled. "Oh, Lana. You have no idea. I'm one of the richest women in the world. I love what I do, and I love the people I work with. How many people you know can say the same?"

Jake interrupted then. "Ms. Marcherand, it's time for you to get ready for the show."

"Thank you, Mr. Wells. Lana, if you'd like to stay, I'd be happy to comp you for the first show. Maybe we could continue this between shows tonight?"

The reporter's eyebrows rose. "I thought you were only doing one show tonight."

Evie shrugged. "Things happen. We were asked, and are pleased to help out. It seemed the nice thing to do, wouldn't you say?"

"Yes." The other woman turned off her recorder and slipped it into her purse. "Thank you. I'd appreciate a chance to see you perform, and I'd love to talk to you between shows if you think you can spare the time." She rose, and so did Evie. They shook hands.

"Bear, would you see Lana out?"

"My pleasure," the big man rumbled. "This way, Ms. Kirkland."

"Lana, please," she said as they moved off.

"I'm off to get some food." Reid stood, stretched. "Jimmy? What about you?"

"Yeah, I could eat. The Pizza Lounge or the buffet?"

"Pizza. It's fresher."

"Point." The two ambled out.

Evie jumped up from her chair, buzzing with energy, her nausea gone. "Ye gods. Did that woman have an agenda, or was she fishing? Does she know, or doesn't she?" She hopped up onto the stage and paced.

Jake took to the stage and came toward her. "You did well."

Evie chewed on her fingernail. "I don't know. She knows something. You know that part about my notebooks? The spiral kind, college ruled? I used those in junior high. At this point, only Brad and Ted would remember that. I haven't touched one since—oh my God." Stricken, she slapped both hands over her mouth.

"What?" Jake gently moved her hands away from her face.

"I just remembered." Her heart thumped. "I haven't listened to Brad's music in, man. Forever. His first hit single sounded a lot like one of my songs, and I was bitter because I didn't get to sing it with him. We'd worked on it together, you see, so it made sense that he'd remember enough of it to make it work. I guess he must have taken the notebook. Damn it. He helped me look for it."

"I'll do some more digging, call Conway, that sort of thing and we'll get this all figured out. I promise." Jake held his arms open and Evie walked into them. Breathed deep. He smelled like fresh air and clean male and the darkest sin imaginable. Comfort and fierce need bubbled up inside her.

She lifted her head and kissed his throat. "I want you." Heat beat a slow burn through her body.

He ran his hand down her back, cupped her ass, and nuzzled her throat. "When you're done. You've got to get ready for the show."

"I've got time." She went up on tiptoe, nipped his ear with her teeth. Soothed it with a kiss. "But I'd much rather spend some time relaxing with you, deep inside me." She tugged on his tie. "Come on."

CHAPTER ELEVEN

Despite everything that had happened, Evie tore up the stage during her first show and the audience ate it up. There was a younger crowd here tonight, Jake noticed, and he wondered whether the positive or the negative parts of that whole social media thing had drawn them in. Not that it mattered. They were here.

She came back for the last couple of songs at the end of her set, surprisingly wearing the pink tee shirt, yellow short overalls, and pink tennis shoes that she'd worn for the interview. The crowd hooted and hollered and she laughed a little breathlessly.

Jake saw Lana Kirkland's eyebrows rise, and her pen flew across her notebook.

"I hope you don't mind the costume change," Evie said, and the house stilled. "The dresses are gorgeous, but this is the real me. I want to thank you all for coming out here on a Tuesday night. I'm changing things up just a little bit, so the guys will be sitting this one out. Want to sing you a song about the man who saved my life. I think you know him. His name is Mike Harper."

The crowd roared their approval. "We love Mike," someone yelled out, and the crowd laughed.

"I love Mike, too." She perched on the stool and picked up her guitar. "This is the first guitar Mike ever bought me. He said that since I was determined to play, I might as well have a damn fine instrument to play on, so he bought me this Taylor GS." She strummed it. "He was one of the guiding influences in my life, and I will always hold him in the highest regard. I wrote this when we knew he was dying, and all we could do was hold on. Mike, this one's for you."

A hush settled over the crowd as Evie strummed her guitar. Then she began picking the notes, and a lilting, lovely melody came out.

"Stubborn and wild and reckless and scared/We laughed and we sang and we pushed and we dared/Till finally truth rapped us hard on the head/Our world came tumbling down/And you said to me/My friend, there's no time to cry/I've got too much living to do/My friend, stand by my side/Help me see it through/I know I've never told you but/You're the best thing I've ever done/My friend,

hold on I'm not ready to go/My friend, hold on let's sing one more song/Oh my girl, hold on tight/Hold on..."

Jake hadn't heard this song before, but it brought an ache to his throat. As she sang, he glanced around and saw more than one tear being wiped away. No one could doubt her honesty, or her talent. Not after hearing this song.

As she finished, there was a hush. Then the audience rose to its feet and the applause filled the club, with patrons whistling and hollering their approval.

"Thank you. Thank you so much. I've got another one for you, and this one's about the first time we met." She swung into the driving beat of "Soul Savior."

"Life on the streets/well it ain't so pretty/dodging the beats/fighting the johns/so I made my way/to Ocean City/the sand was so warm and/the waves were a song."

Jake's phone vibrated in his pocket. He slipped out into the hallway and listened to the message from Conway.

"Positive tweets coming out tonight. By the way, the band's YouTube channel is up, so please tell them. Nothing yet from Bradley Gaines' manager, and I've been using pressure. We aren't friends, but we do know each other, and have a lot of acquaintances in common. I'll keep in touch."

Jake pocketed his phone, wishing for just five minutes alone with Bradley Gaines. Reining in his anger, he headed back into the club and stood in the rear, watching Evie hold the audience captive.

He felt a kinship with the audience, as he'd been her captive earlier as she straddled him, sitting in the only chair in the small dressing room. He remained clothed, but since she'd had to change anyway, she stripped for him. Gave him a lap dance that went way beyond dancing.

Man. He discreetly adjusted himself, mentally scolding his cock for acting like a randy teenager. Back then, looking at any girl had gotten him hard. Now, his focus was solely and completely on her. She pulled his trigger.

It had never been like this before.

The roar of the audience brought him back to the present.

"Thank you, and goodnight!"

The stage lights dimmed as the house lights came up. Before he could move, he found himself stalked.

Lana Kirkland had him in her sights, and it didn't look like he'd be getting away from her. He sighed, determined to make the best of it.

Those watchful eyes made her smile look sly as she came toward him, swaying on sky-high heels. "Mr. Wells, was it? I assume you're the club manager? We weren't introduced earlier."

"That's right, we weren't introduced." Seeing no need to set her straight about his employment, Jake kept his slightly bored social mask in place. The aisles streamed with people leaving, the chatter factor high and excited.

"I thought," Lana said, her voice dropping to an intimate level so that Jake had to lean forward to hear her, "that you were my best bet to make sure I get to talk to Evie."

He clasped his hands behind him. "She said she'd talk to you, so she will. She keeps her word, Ms. Kirkland."

The woman pouted. "The girl is beginning to sound like a paragon. She nurses a lush like Mike Harper through AIDS, she can sing and write songs, and she keeps her word. Good lord, how boring."

Jake kept rein on his temper. "If you have other obligations this evening, I'm sure Evie will understand."

Her eyes narrowed. "And let this ripe little story get away from me? Not a chance. Us working stiffs have it tough, not like this little cookie. But that's all right. If she won't talk to me, I know someone who will."

"Ms. Kirkland. She will be here." He turned the full weight of his disapproval toward her and she took a step back, tapped her hand against her thigh in a nervous beat.

The club had pretty much cleared out by that time, leaving the wait staff to clean up. Lana moved restlessly. "Damn smoking laws," she muttered.

Jake took the opportunity to escape. He spied a table toward the front, already bussed and wiped down. "Come, have a seat. Can I get you anything? A glass of wine? Bottle of water?" He put a hand in the small of her back and urged her forward.

"Well. Just water." She sat and looked up at him expectantly. "Then we can talk."

He raised an eyebrow. "I'll be right back." Stopping a passing waiter, he requested the bottle of water before making a beeline backstage. He knocked at her dressing room door and let himself in, shutting the door swiftly behind him.

Evie was using a washcloth to wipe down her body. She stood there, gloriously naked, humming a happy little ditty that he'd never heard before, her show makeup already refreshed.

She grinned over her shoulder at him, tossed the washcloth in the sink, took the three steps to his side and drew his head down for a kiss. "I'm so glad that was you who walked in while I was naked."

"Me, too." He kissed her again, his hands on her waist. "Don't forget Lana. By the way, she thinks I'm an employee of the hotel. She's out for blood, babe."

Evie pursed her lips. "Well." She slipped out of his reach, pulled the red dress on over her head. "I'm not surprised. Blood, after all, is so much more interesting than anything happy, don't you think? I decided I'm not going to run scared. I haven't done anything to be ashamed of."

"I'm pretty sure she knows how to get to Bradley, too. She said if you weren't going to talk, she knew someone who would." He leaned against the door, enjoying watching her pull her siren-red thong underwear up her legs before fluffing her skirt back down.

"Aren't you just full of good news?" She slid on her red heels. "If you're a hotel flunky, then can I have you bring me one slice of pizza? And a bottle of water?"

"Absolutely." He leaned down, kissed her hard. "I'll go out ahead of you, get that taken care of. Let her stew another five minutes before you make your entrance."

She grinned up at him. "Can do."

"I know you can." He gave her another kiss and her hand tightened around his neck as she deepened the kiss. He pulled away, dazed, and shook his head. "You're lethal."

"Me? No one has ever said that about me before," she said, patently delighted. Her tummy rumbled and they both laughed. "Go, get me pizza," she ordered, pointing at the door. "Then rescue me."

"Will do."

Jake took care to wipe the silly grin off his face as he left her.

He used his phone as a prop as he crossed the stage, gave Lana a nod, and headed to the bar in back, where he found a waitress cleaning up. "Can you help me out," he checked her name tag, "Maisie? Evie needs a medium pizza, pepperoni and extra cheese.

And we need it in about twenty minutes." He leaned on the bar and did his best to be charming. It wasn't too difficult. Maisie, in her late thirties he guessed, had a country-sweetheart look about her.

Maisie grinned. "For you, handsome? Of course. That girl of yours, wow. She's a stunner all right. I've watched each one of her shows."

"Thanks. I think so, too. You're a life saver, Maisie." He handed her some cash. "Here you go, and keep the change."

She batted her lashes, smiled hopefully. "Think I can get her autograph?"

"Of course. And how about a picture? We can arrange that. You come in with the pizza, and we'll take the picture." He patted her hand. "I've got to make sure the reporter in there doesn't eat her alive. Which is why the pizza is important," he reminded her.

Maisie nodded. "I'm on it. I'll call it in right now." She turned to the phone behind the bar and Jake took a moment to check his Twitter feed. Evie's hashtag filled his phone, and it looked mostly positive.

So far, so good.

* * *

Evie had answered the reporter's rather innocuous questions. As each one passed, she relaxed a little more.

"And you were born, where?"

"El Cajon, California. Right next to San Diego."

"So, it's just us girls here now. Tell me, are you involved with anyone? In a relationship, I mean?"

Evie smiled and looked down at her fingers. "A lady never tells."

"What about your first love, Bradley Gaines? What does he think about your career?

"Brad doesn't…oh, you're good." Evie sat back and eyed the shark opposite her. The woman had an insolent sneer on her face.

"Do you refuse to answer the question?"

Evie folded her hands together to keep from snatching up the recorder between them and bashing it against the wall. "As I was going to say, I haven't seen nor talked to Brad in eleven years. I doubt seriously that he thinks about *my* career at all. Especially since

I'm just a beginner, and he's a star." Even as she said the words, her heart ached.

She thought she'd gotten over his betrayal. Apparently she was wrong. She refocused on Lana, who had asked another question.

"I'm sorry, I missed that. Could you repeat it, please?"

Lana raised an eyebrow. "I said, you have more of a career than what you've done here at the Four Parrots. The band's YouTube channel is exploding. That last song you sang, The 'Soul Savior'? It's gotten a quarter of a million hits already, and it just got posted today."

Evie's jaw dropped. "Is that good? Of course it's good, but I mean. Is that a good thing?" She turned to Jake, standing against the far wall. "Jake?"

"It's good. Your manager called while you were on stage earlier, and I haven't had a chance to tell you the news. Thank you, Maisie," he added, as the waitress brought over a piping hot pizza. "Ms. Kirkland, I apologize, but your time with Ms. Marcherand has just run out. She has to get ready for the next show." Jake ushered Lana out with charm, flustering the reporter so much she dropped her digital recorder.

Evie's stomach lurched at the scent of the melted cheese and Italian spices. What had she been thinking? "Maisie?" She hated the weakness in her voice.

"What's up, sweetie?" The waitress came over, tucking her hair behind her ears.

Evie pushed the pizza away. "I can't eat this right now. After the show, yes, but not right now."

The woman nodded sympathetically. "You want some pink stuff? You know, the stuff that helps with upset stomachs?" Maisie looked around and lowered her voice. "Pepto. I've got some, if you want it."

The answer to her prayers. "Yes, please."

Maisie patted Evie's shoulder. "You stay right there. I'll take care of this, and get a fresh pizza sent to your room after the next show. Your man tipped me plenty to take care of you, so I will. Be right back with the Pepto." She whisked the pizza away.

"He's not my—oh hell." Evie frowned, watching the waitress head to the small kitchen behind the bar. "My man," she said, tasting the words. They felt funny in her mouth.

Jake came back and frowned when he saw she wasn't eating. "No pizza?"

"Queasy stomach," Evie confessed. "I just couldn't. Maisie said she'd send another one up after the second show."

He studied her face. "You've gone real pale. Did Lana upset you? I heard her ask about Brad."

Evie's temples throbbed. "No. Yes. I don't know. Damn it. Maybe I've caught a bug, or something. I'll bet you're ready to go to Spain right about now," she joked.

"What are you thinking that's got you so upset?" Jake reached across the table, took her hand and held it. "Care to share?"

The tenderness in his voice made her heart ache. "You've been wonderful this week. I want you to know that. I mean, you've been great." She caught sight of Maisie, the pink bottle discreet behind a napkin. "Excuse me. I need to do some meditation before the next show." She stood and turned away.

On shaky legs, she went to take the Pepto for her stomach. This being a performer had twists to it she hadn't seen coming.

CHAPTER TWELVE

The drive to Scottsdale, Arizona the next day seemed to take forever. Reid and Jimmy kept everyone up to date on the social media chatter until it all became too much for Evie. She went to the back of the bus where Jake sat reading and pulled out her guitar, needing to lose herself in her music. She stifled a sigh as she watched Jake read. He wore dark trousers and a light blue, button-down shirt with the shirtsleeves rolled up his forearm.

She shook her head. What was wrong with blue jeans and a tee shirt?

Trying to ignore him, she noodled a little bit on the guitar. The sound was getting thin, which meant it was time to change some of her guitar strings. At least that was a normal thing she could do. She sighed and reached over to pull out a packet of strings from her guitar case.

"You keep sighing." Jake put his magazine down. "Sighing is a sign of needing mental stimulation. You're a sigher."

"I'm not a sigher, and I have plenty of mental stimulation." Deftly, she unwound the lowest string from the tuning peg. She tugged at the bridge pin at the other end until it came off, and pulled the string free.

"Not only are you sighing, but you've been very quiet since we left Las Vegas this morning. Actually, you've been quiet since after the second show last night. Care to share what's going on in that head of yours?"

He had phrased the question casually, but she took it as anything but. She frowned, took a soft cloth and polished the area where the string normally lay. "Nothing is going on. My head is as empty as a whiskey bottle in an alcoholic's recycle bin." She kept her focus on the guitar, not wanting to see the probing look in his eyes.

"Why don't I believe that?"

Evie clamped her mouth shut. With care, she pulled out the new string from the package and uncoiled it. Settled the ball end into the hole in the bridge and replaced the pin.

"Hello. Earth to Evie, come in, Evie."

Calmly, she met the curiosity in his gaze. "I'm fine. I'm also busy. I don't want to talk. I have two shows to do, there's a ton of publicity out there about me by people who don't know me, and I find that very strange. I just want to sit back here and change a couple of guitar strings. Okay?"

She suffered through his careful study of her face without showing how close she was to losing it completely.

"Okay." He stood up, his face now blank. "I'll just go up front. Let you have some privacy."

As he left, Evie blinked back tears. Nothing about this tour was going as she had expected. From the dingy dressing rooms to exploring Jake, and everything that had happened in between. She should never have pursued Jake. She never should have kissed him on the beach, never should have had those intimate talks in the dark, and never, ever should have made love with him.

She needed to stand on her own two feet and remember how it felt. She needed to grab her life and live it, ride this career as far as it would take her. To do that, she needed to be free to absorb the many changes going on without criticism or expectation from anyone other than the guys in the band.

Thoughts churning, she finished attaching the six string. The whole social media thing freaked her out. People she'd never met had now heard her sing on YouTube. Jimmy had been kind enough to show her how the site YouTube worked. He also showed her their video and she was pleased, if still perplexed. People she didn't know were sharing the video, talking about her and the band on Twitter, holding all sorts of discussions on Facebook about her. It was exciting and scary, all mixed up. She didn't need Jake telling her how she should really dive into Twitter and Facebook.

Okay, so Johnny M, the Beast, had dropped more clues this morning on his blog about the "insider" calling her a fake. But she didn't need Jake to be all sympathetic. She could handle it, if he left her alone.

She sighed. It was only Wednesday. Had they really started this adventure only four days ago?

She had tonight free, then two shows in Scottsdale on Thursday, then a day to travel to Los Angeles. One show there, and then she could go home, a mere two-hour jaunt down the coast. By Sunday at the latest, she'd be home.

Home. Evie replaced the three string while she thought about the lovely beach cottage in San Diego that Mike had left to her. With him gone, it was just a place. A very pretty place, to be sure, and one she would always have fond memories of, but that place was the home of her past. The home of her coming-of-age.

Before that, though, San Diego had been the place she'd fallen for her first knight in shining armor. She'd never forget Brad coming to rescue six-year-old Evie. She owed him, and if the price she needed to pay were those songs he'd taken, so many years ago, then so be it. He could have the songs, but he couldn't have her reputation. That was non-negotiable. Surely there was some way to work it all out.

A decade was a long time to hold a torch and a longer time to hold a grudge. She'd love to talk to Brad, check up on him, see how he was doing. Okay, and maybe see if there was any love left inside her for him. But he'd made his choice years ago, and it hadn't been her.

She shook her head as she tuned the guitar. What an idiot she was. Of course she wasn't still in love with Brad. She had far too much pride to run after a man who had discarded her. If that had been her plan, she'd have done it back when she was fifteen.

No. Brad wasn't for her. He could have her songs, if indeed he'd ever done anything with her notebook. But she couldn't allow him to ruin her reputation and her career before it truly got started. Maybe Conway could get in touch with Brad, so they could at least talk. The stuff circulating about her was ridiculous. If, of course, it actually was Brad behind it all.

If it was, then once Brad and his activities were out of the way, she'd be able to see clearly what to do about Jake. Right now, everything was too muddled, what with her career, Brad, the rumors, Mike. There was a lot standing between them, and she needed to tackle it all first.

"You're everything I didn't know I needed/Everything I long for/Everything I dream…"

Evie's heart thumped and she shook her head in denial. She would never call Jake her dream man. He was stuffy, not to mention bossy. But somehow his stuffiness had become endearing. Physically, they were definitely a match. Last night had proved that, once again.

But the bossy, overprotective part of him made her wonder if, perhaps, she was just a job to him. After all, he hadn't said anything to the contrary. There was nothing, bar that first kiss, that made her believe that he saw her as anything more than a job. An important one, a promise made to a dying man, but still just a job. She was the one who dangled the stupid expiration date in front of him. Of course he'd take her up on it. Sex for a week with no strings? What man wouldn't?

It would be nice to have someone put her first for a change. She straightened her spine. Of course, it was past time she put herself first, which was what this tour was all about. Yes, Mike had arranged everything in advance, and yes Conway was managing it all, but still. This tour was hers, not theirs.

Which made the social media stuff make sense. Somehow. Her career was about her, not about her and some man. It was all about *her*. Right? Frowning, she finger-picked the notes to "House of the Rising Sun" and contemplated her future.

Rhoads came over the loudspeaker. "Scottsdale. Five minutes to the hotel."

Evie set her guitar in its case and stretched, avid for her first glance at the new city. That was a huge perk to this lifestyle, she mused. Getting out and about and seeing the country, not tied any more to one city or state. Eager now, she headed to the front of the bus.

***

Jake leaned against the headboard and listened to the faint sounds of Evie's guitar through the thin walls of the hotel. She was everything he'd never known he wanted. How was he supposed to make her fall in love with him if he couldn't keep her with him? Because one thing he'd decided, while watching her on stage tonight, was that there was no way in hell he would let her go. Not now. He'd tried to talk himself out of it. He'd fallen hard, and much too fast, which scared the shit out of him. She was too young, talented as hell, and she'd be on the road forever. Her career would always come first, and it deserved to come first.

Mercurial. God, he'd never known a woman to change emotions as quickly as she did. Her goofy side was endearing, and yet something about her hinted at depths of knowledge and feeling that weren't apparent at first glance.

And then, too, she was so damn sexy. He got lost, sometimes, watching her, listening to her. His body hardened even now, thinking of her. Of the way she was with him, the way they were together. She was like all his teenaged fantasies come true, only better. Remembering the sight of her mouth on his cock and the pleasure she'd taken in pleasuring him, had him groaning as he grew even harder. Had anyone ever fit him so well?

He sighed. Three in the morning and neither one of them could sleep. If they were in the same damn room, they'd have taken the edge off with a healthy bout of sex and would be snoring like children at this point.

Something was bugging her, despite her earlier denial. She'd been mesmerizing during her shows that night, and it all had to do with her emotional state. When she was happy, she glowed. But during her set she'd been wistful, and even the hard-driving songs had given him a catch in his throat. He hadn't been alone in that, either, as the band had crowded around her between shows, which they didn't normally do.

He thought back to earlier, when they'd first arrived in Scottsdale and at the hotel. He never should have suggested separate rooms. He wouldn't have if his own fear hadn't brought it up, and he never expected her to agree to it. He scowled at the painting of two ducks in a pond that graced the wall opposite him.

Her agreeing pissed him off. She wasn't supposed to want separate rooms, damn it. A knock on the connecting door had him scrambling for his jeans. He pushed his hair off his forehead and opened the door.

Evie stood there, in pale blue silk nothings, storm warnings in her dark eyes. "I am not a child."

Surprised, he raised an eyebrow. "This theme keeps coming up. I've never thought of you as a child."

She pushed her way into his room and paced from one side to the other, her agitation making her movements unusually jerky. "Mike gave me to you. You're just a substitute for Mike. That's all this is. Pure emotional transference."

Anger slowly simmered inside him. "You know that's not true. Whatever you may feel for me has nothing to do with Mike. Our connection on the beach proves that."

She narrowed her eyes. "You put sunscreen on me. In public."

"Two days ago. And you laughed at me." Jake had to use all his control not to pick her up and devour her, one silky inch of skin at a time.

"You wear suits," she pointed out. "And you're always giving me advice."

He breathed slowly, determined to keep his hands to himself. "The suits get the job done, and you can always ignore the advice."

"You're cool and in control all the time, and it doesn't matter to you that we're in separate rooms. It's killing me that we're in separate rooms. It killed me that you suggested separate rooms." She stopped in front of him, her cheeks bright with color and her breath heavy with emotion. "You know what else I'm not? I'm not your sister. I'm a woman, God help me, with a huge crush on you. It's driving me crazy and it's not fair."

"Isn't crush kind of a high school word?" He had to inject a little humor into the situation, or he was going to explode.

"Don't make light of this," she snapped, her hands on her hips. "I want you gone. I don't need you here, messing me up, going hot and cold. You're making me crazy and I can't concentrate and I can't write and I can't—"

In a desperate attempt to soothe them both, he yanked her to him and kissed her, his anger and anxiety at her summary dismissal melting as she kissed him back, fiercely. Their tongues fought in a wild mating that mimicked what he needed from her. Her hands grabbed onto him, held as he lifted her, and with three quick strides he had her on the bed.

Without breaking their kiss, he shucked off his jeans, pulled down her shorts. Then, finally, he stepped back, his hands on his hips, his eyes hard. "Tell me you want me to leave."

She licked her lips, her gaze darting down to his erect cock before looking back up at him. "Stay." Her pulse pounded through her body, her sex drenched. She stripped off her top and lay back on the bed, one hand going to her wetness. "Please." She spread her legs wide in invitation.

He grabbed a condom, sheathed himself and knelt between her legs, slowly lowering his chest until it met hers. "You are a sexy wench. You are maddening and sweet and however long we're together, I will never get enough of you." He plunged into her then and she cried out his name.

Evie opened to him, held nothing back. She licked and bit his shoulder, loving the taste of him, then wrapped her legs around his waist and urged him on in their race for completion.

He bent down to suckle her nipple. He tugged, and she shrieked, her orgasm hitting fast and strong. Her body rippled with it, tightened around him until mere seconds later, he came and buried his face in her neck as his passion emptied out of him.

They lay together, their hearts beating a crazy rhythm, their breathing harsh as energies from their passion sparked and rippled across their bodies.

"Ah, hell." She hadn't meant for them to end up here. Or had she? Evie pushed the thought away, not having the energy to dissect her motives.

"You do angry sex well." He murmured in her ear, sending shivers across her body.

"Mm. So do you."

She felt Jake lifting up on his elbows and turned his way. He took her mouth in a deep—and deeply satisfying—kiss.

"I'll be right back. Don't go anywhere," he warned.

"I'll be here."

He was back before her body had cooled down. He pulled up the covers around them and settled her against him, her head on his shoulder and his hand firmly on her ass. "Maybe now we can get some sleep."

Evie smiled in the dark. "We need to talk," she said on a yawn.

"You may not be exhausted, but I am. We have all day tomorrow to talk. Okay?"

"Okay. Since you asked so sweetly." She snuggled down into the covers, into him. She loved curling up next to him, their still-damp bodies cooling, the scent of the two of them in the air. Evie floated on hazy delight.

She was almost asleep when Jake spoke again.

"Thank you."

"Mm. For what?"

"For knocking on the door. I needed this."

She kissed his collarbone, wide awake now. "Thank you for opening the door." She didn't say another word but stared long into the dark and wondered how she could possibly be so stupidly close to falling in love. Wondered, with a kind of panic, what she could do to stop it from happening.

CHAPTER THIRTEEN

Jake handed over his cell phone. "Talk to Conway."

Evie frowned and looked up from her downward dog pose. Jake's voice had gotten really tight while he'd been talking to her manager. She brought her knees down to the floor and reached for the phone. "Yeah, Conway. What's up?"

"You settled in to the hotel okay?"

"The Sportsman's Lodge is very nice. Lots of room for the bus, too." She rolled her eyes and looked toward Jake, but he wouldn't meet her gaze. "Are you coming to the Topaz Room tomorrow?"

"Wouldn't miss it. Which is why I'm calling."

Evie waited, but the man didn't say anything. "Conway? Are you there?"

"You see, it's like this. Bradley Gaines is in town, and he'd like to come talk to you."

Evie caught her breath and sent a swift, seeking look to Jake. His eyes were a brilliant blue, and his face didn't give away his thoughts.

"Evie?"

"I'm thinking. Give me a few seconds." It was what she had wanted, the chance to talk to Brad. Should she ask Jake? But if she asked Jake, it would be deferring to someone else. This was her life, right? But then again, she and Jake were, well, lovers, to put it bluntly. Shouldn't she ask his opinion?

"When did he want to meet?" She turned away from Jake and went to the window, which overlooked the sparkling pool.

"This afternoon."

"Will you be here?"

"I'm about forty minutes away, depending on traffic. Yes, I'll be there."

She leaned against the window, the glass only faintly cool against her skin. "Okay. I'll meet him. But you and I need to talk before he ever shows up."

"It's almost one-thirty now. I'll call you when I get in and we'll talk. How about we set the meeting for four? We'll take it in my suite," he added. Then suddenly he started yelling. "Damn stupid

Audi driver. Stay in your own lane, you fecking bastard. Oh hell, a cop. Bye, Evie. See you soon."

Evie handed the phone back to Jake. "Conway is now getting a ticket for driving while on the phone. Before that, he was about forty minutes away."

Jake's eyebrows rose. "Serves him right. So how do you feel about seeing Brad again?"

"Nothing like cutting to the chase, is there?" Restless, she settled back into the yoga routine that the phone conversation had interrupted. "I don't know. Don't really want to think about it right now. Ask me again when I'm finished here."

She moved through the stretches and poses easily, tried her best to slow her breathing. How *did* she feel about seeing Brad again, after all these years? She tried on various emotions, but none of them seemed to fit. She'd once loved him. He'd left her without warning or explanation, even a note, but she'd gotten tired of holding onto that grudge. She wouldn't mind seeing her old friend, the kid who had saved her life by taking her under his wing more than once.

On the other hand, if he turned out to be her stalker, then she'd be white-hot pissed off.

Sifting through the pieces of her past as she worked out, she still had a hard time making Brad the villain. Whether it was because he had been such an influence during her younger years, or because he'd been her first lover, she couldn't be totally sure.

She built up a sweat during her yoga workout and tried to plan her day. Meet with Conway. Meet with Brad. Go to dinner with Jake and have a come-to-Jesus talk with him about the future of their relationship. She needed to hammer home that expiration date before she found herself in any deeper. Once they hit San Diego, they were over. Her stomach rolled at the thought and she struggled to regain her inner balance.

"Oh, hell, he didn't." Jake's voice interrupted her concentration.

Evie rose from plank position to a downward dog, brought her feet up to where her hands lay flat on the floor, and slowly stood to face Jake, who was tapping on his computer.

"What's wrong now?" She lifted her arms over her head and began a round of sun salutations.

"The Beast of Social Media has spilled the beans. He named his source."

She patted the floor with her hands, rose back up to a standing position, and walked over to where Jake sat. "Who is it?"

His gaze met hers, and she knew. "Bradley." Pain slashed her heart and slowly faded. This betrayal was almost worse than the first one he'd dealt her, so long ago. Even though The Beast had named Brad, it didn't feel right. Maybe she just didn't want to believe it.

Jake's cell phone buzzed. After a brief conversation that Evie didn't follow, he sighed and hung up. "Conway's here. Meet him at the pool bar. He's stopping there before he goes up to his room. Says he needs a beer."

"He's not the only one." Aware of Jake's concerned gaze, she shrugged. "I'll be fine. We'll get to the bottom of this. Do me a favor when Brad arrives?"

"I'll be happy to," he said, cracking his knuckles and rubbing his hands. "My pleasure."

"No. God, no, don't beat him up," she said. A chuckle broke through, despite her best efforts. "Not that I wouldn't kind of enjoy it." She went to him, pressed close and put her hands on his shoulders. Held his gaze. "What I don't want is for you or Conway to take over. This is my fight, not yours. I don't want you to talk for me, or make threats for me, or in any way step on my conversation with Brad."

She met his skeptical gaze. "Grown woman standing here," she reminded him, and pressed her hand against his cheek.

He sighed, bent to kiss her forehead then wrapped his arms around her. "Am I allowed to jump in front of you if he starts waving a gun or a knife around?"

"In case of possible injury to my body, you may absolutely jump in and take over. But that's not going to happen. Brad's not like that. He's never been like that."

"Evie. He is smearing your good name. That's all you have right now."

She sent him a cocky smile. "That, talent, a house in San Diego, and friends. I'm a rich woman, Jake Wells. Didn't you know? So promise me."

He stared at her face for so long without answering that for a moment, she thought perhaps he was gearing up for an argument. To her relief, he nodded. "I promise. This is your issue to handle, but I'm not going to be far from your side. I stick with you."

She frowned.

"Those are my terms. Take it or leave it." His tone told her she'd better take it.

Evie sighed. "Taking it. I'm off to see Conway." She gave him a quick kiss and headed out, giddy at getting his agreement.

***

Telling Conway everything about her life with Brad felt a little like what she imagined confessing to a priest must feel like. He just steepled his fingers, tapped his lips, and nodded whenever she'd run out of things to say, which prompted her to say more. But at least now he was on board with her strategy, which was to first figure out *if* Brad was the stalker, and if he wasn't, to smoke out the real stalker using the both of them as bait. Because if Brad wasn't the stalker, someone from their shared past had to be. That was the only thing that made any sense to her. And that was a very short list.

Now, an hour later, Evie stared at the clothes hanging in the closet. What did you wear to meet the rat bastard who, just possibly, was trying to ruin your career before it ever got started?

She stiffened her spine. Weakness was for sissies. Long ago when Brad had rescued her she'd been young and defenseless, but she'd never been weak, and now was not the time to start. She flicked through her clothes until she found the perfect outfit. A bit unusual, perhaps, but then again, these were unusual circumstances. A quick glance at the clock on the bedside table told her she had time to do it right. Humming, she headed to the bathroom. First, a long, steamy bath. Then, fragrant lotion.

Next? The killer outfit. Conway's plan was pure genius, if they could pull it off. It would all depend on Brad. Mentally crossing her fingers, Evie prepared for the performance of her life.

***

Jake paced in front of the wide window in the living area of Conway's suite. "Are you sure you know what you're doing?"

"Hell no. But Evie is set on this course, and Brad seemed sincere. Don't worry. It's not like we're going to leave the two of them alone," he added wryly.

The thought knotted Jake's stomach. "Not for a second." He pulled his phone from his pocket. "It's almost four. Where's Evie?"

"She'll be here." Conway, hunched over his laptop, tapped away at the keys. "Stop worrying. We've got it all planned, and I'm certain we're on the right track. I just had to play that sleazeball Johnny M's game, but in the long run we'll come out on top. So, like I said. Stop worrying."

"I've been worrying about her since the first minute I saw her in the moonlight at the wake." Jake spun around, pointed at Conway and scowled. "I didn't just say that."

Conway raised his eyebrows. "The moonlight? Really."

Jake thrust his hands in his pockets. "The wake. Moonlight and waves and her electric-blue bikini. I should have known better than to make an appearance."

Con sat back and steepled his fingers, covering up a grin. "Moonlight. Bikinis. I can see how it would be a worrying experience."

Jake rubbed his temple where a headache threatened. "She's too young for me. She's got this great career just waiting for her to grab it. She'll be traveling for years."

Conway chuckled. "Jake, my man, who exactly are you talking to? And what the hell are you trying to say?"

"Does it matter? As soon as we hit San Diego, it's over."

A knock came at the door. The two men looked at each other.

"I'll get it." Jake moved to open it.

On the other side of the door was the face he'd love to smash with his fist. Bradley Gaines. He took a deep breath and stepped aside. "Come in."

The man nodded respectfully—the damn pup—and passed him, looking around the room eagerly. "Where is she?"

Jake shut the door. Conway stood.

"I'm Conway Davis, her agent, and this is Jake Wells. Evie's running a little late, but she'll be here. Would you like a drink?"

"No, thanks. Just got out of rehab." He shrugged, a carelessly graceful gesture.

Jake watched the man with narrowed eyes. He had burnished brown hair, a chiseled face, brown eyes. A little soft around the middle, he noted with some satisfaction. He tuned into the man's mild drawl as he tried to butter up Conway.

"Thanks for arranging this meeting. I really appreciate it."

Conway nodded. "Have a seat. You understand we won't be leaving you alone with Evie."

Brad looked from one man to another and sighed. "I suppose I deserve that. She's told you, then?"

Silent, Jake just leaned against the wall and folded his arms.

Conway sat again. "She'll be here in a minute. Unless you have something you want to confess before that?"

"Confess?" Confusion crossed his face. "I don't get it. Is something wrong?"

Jake snorted. Conway sent him a warning glance. Jake spoke up anyway.

"Why don't you just sit there and keep your mouth shut until Evie gets here. You can do your talking then."

Brad gulped and sat in one of the two chairs opposite the couch. "I hope she hurries up," he muttered.

Another knock sounded. Jake moved to open the door.

Evie stood there, her chin lifted and fire in her eyes. "I'll talk to you later," she promised, jabbing him in the chest with her forefinger.

He bit back the words on his lips and stood aside for her to enter, even as his instincts screamed at him to cover her up.

She wore one of her silk sleep tanks, this one in a deep pink, and hadn't bothered with a bra. It topped a short, swirly, flirty skirt in a forest green, and she wore pale pink high tops on her feet. She looked like a beautiful rose, and he wanted to scoop her up and undress her. Slowly.

Instead, he took his place by the wall and watched as Brad's face lit up. He bounced from his chair and came toward her, his arms wide.

Jealousy dug deep in Jake's gut, but it eased a bit when he saw Evie put her hands up to stop his advance. Brad halted about three feet away from her. Admiration shone in his eyes.

"Evie. You, wow. You're all grown up."

"It happens. Sometimes it happens very fast. Like when your best friend in the entire world runs away, taking his brother with him but leaving you behind. How is Ted, by the way?"

Brad took a step back from her anger. "Come on. That was years ago."

"That doesn't make it any less devastating to the fifteen-year-old me."

"But you look great. I love your YouTube videos. Wow, you finally grew into your voice, right? Please, sit."

Jake watched as Evie, practically vibrating with anger, took a seat next to Conway on the couch.

She came right to the point. "Why are you here, Brad?"

"Because we haven't seen each other in years. Because, oh, so many reasons. I've missed you."

"Took you long enough to find me." She crossed her arms.

He shifted uncomfortably. "Come on, Evie. Be fair. It's not as though you're on Facebook or Twitter. And yeah, I looked."

Jake had had enough. He strolled forward so he could see both Brad and Evie's faces. "Let's cut to the chase, Bradley. You wanted to see Evie, but we had a reason of our own for having you here. Why the attempts to ruin Evie's reputation?"

The look of shock on Brad's face almost convinced him of his innocence. "I don't understand."

Conway intervened. "Johnny M, the Beast of All Social Media, outed you today as his source for the libelous tweets he's been putting out this week."

Brad swallowed hard. "It wasn't me."

"Just confess, Brad. Make it easy on everyone. Confess, and don't do it again, and I won't press charges. But I will require you to retract everything you've said to Johnny M." Determination shone in Evie's face.

"Evie. You know me," he pleaded. "I wouldn't do anything to you. *Especially* not to you. What was so terrible? What did Johnny M do?" At Evie's look of incomprehension, he added, "I just got out of rehab last night. Six months sober," he added.

"Why should I believe you? Why did you contact me, today of all days?" The hurt rang in her voice, and it made Jake hurt, too.

Brad looked from one antagonistic face to the other. "Just got out of rehab yesterday, like I said. Six months. I stayed away from social media. Haven't seen or talked to a reporter the entire time. I finally got custody of my iPhone again and saw your name pop up on my Twitter feed. A link to YouTube. Man, Evie. You totally rocked that song. Then Carl called, told me Conway was looking for me. That you were looking for me. Why *wouldn't* I contact you today?"

She chewed on her thumbnail, and Jake could tell she was turning his words over in her mind. "So you didn't give false information to Johnny M?"

"Nope. Never would. I was never into that kind of thing. You know that. Or you once did. I really screwed up with you, didn't I?"

Evie didn't answer. She just sat back and tucked one foot under her. "Well, this kind of puts a different light on things, doesn't it?" She glanced at Conway. "Still want to go through with our plan?"

He rubbed his hands. "Absolutely. Whoever is doing this will be shocked. I can arrange some media coverage, too."

"What plan?" Jake couldn't help but be suspicious. "Why didn't you involve me?"

Conway ignored Jake. "Bradley, how would you like to sing with Evie tomorrow night at the Topaz Room? Yes, it's more a place for newcomers, but they'd welcome you with open arms. And if we drop hints in advance that you'll be there, your first performance out of rehab, they'll definitely sell out."

"I don't like it," Jake growled.

Brad gave him a nervous look. "I'm up for it, as long as Carl, my manager, is okay with it. But why?"

"We need to put the rumors to rest," Evie explained. "If we're seen as being friendly, that'll go a long way to killing the bad stuff. It's why I think it'll work. But I need you to be certain. The rumors involve me stealing songs from you. We both know that isn't true," she added. "But why the focus on plagiarism?"

"Is that what you call it, plagiarism?" Brad laughed. "I can't write songs to save my life," he admitted. He sent a friendly smile toward Conway. "Evie was always the one who wrote the songs. And the lyrics. Even at twelve, she had the gift. Hell, she was always humming and making up songs."

"You'd be willing to testify to that in court?" Jake intercepted a glare from Evie and held his hands out. "I'm just asking."

But Brad was nodding. "Yeah, I'll swear to it. Anything to fix things for Evie. We saved each other, you know, way back when." He sent a soft look to Evie, who waved her hand in dismissal.

"You saved me. I didn't save you," she demurred.

He winked and grinned. "We'll have to agree to disagree. Later, we'll catch up, share notes on our past. How do you want to work this gig tomorrow night?"

Conway pulled out a blank pad of paper, and the other two gathered around.

Jake watched as they talked songs and guitars. Conway called the rest of the band, and soon there were too many people in the room, all speaking an alien language.

He kept to himself while watching Evie. She came alive as the afternoon wore into evening and decisions were made through lots of discussion, argument, and laughter. As time passed, Evie grew more relaxed and comfortable with Brad. Jake had to keep a tight rein on his patience.

Finally, Jimmy and Reid said they were off to find some dinner. Bear shook Brad's hand and gave Evie a kiss on the cheek. They all agreed to meet at noon the next day for a run-through of some songs. Then even Bear was gone, and it was just the four of them again.

"May I ask you something, Brad?" Jake shot a swift look at Evie, who nodded her permission.

A wary glint came into Brad's eyes. "Sure. Fire away."

"While we were researching you, we found out that you've had IRS issues, plus a domestic assault and battery charge. Apparently your bank account isn't doing too well. Oh, and your new CD dropped last week and isn't doing very well, either."

"Jake, really," Evie protested. "Be nice. Brad, do you remember when we went looking for my missing notebook? With all my songs? You know, the week before you took off. I've been wondering. Did you take it?"

Brad paled. "I didn't take that notebook, I swear to God, Evie." He turned to Jake. "I'm not sure what's been going on since I've been in rehab, and I'll have to check with my business manager. Not my talent manager, not Carl, you understand," he said hurriedly to Conway, who nodded. "I need to get in touch with my brother." Brad stood. "While I'd like to continue this over a meal, I'd best be on my way. Sort out my life a bit. I'm not sure how good I'll be at it, since I've screwed up a lot over the years."

Evie stood as well, skirting the coffee table to give him a hug. "Thank you for finding me again," she said, and she stood on tiptoe to press a kiss to his cheek. "I'll buy a cell phone, I promise."

"And you'll keep in touch?" Brad brushed his hand across the top of her head.

"Of course I will. We're practically family."

Jake watched, stone-faced, as she hugged him once more and walked him to the door.

"Thank you again."

Brad grinned, tapped her on the nose. "See you tomorrow, short stuff."

"Beanpole," she shot back with a smile.

Finally she closed the door and practically skipped back to the couch. "Well, that was totally awesome. You know, he hasn't changed that much, but he did get a bit out of shape," she mused. "Maybe his rehab didn't have an exercise program."

Jake kept his mouth shut.

Conway looked at his watch. "It's after eight," he said in surprise. "Is anyone interested in dinner?"

"I'm starving. How about you, Jake?"

"Yep."

"Great. Let's go get us some food, since we're all dressed so pretty," she said. "Conway, you're buying. I am so excited about tomorrow."

"Of course. Lead on, dear girl."

As Conway passed Jake, he shook his head. "Keep it together, man. This is not the time."

Jake followed, wondered how soon he could get Evie alone. She was right. They needed to talk.

CHAPTER FOURTEEN

"You've been broody-bad-moody all through dinner. If there had been a dog around, you'd have kicked it. Having that talk with Brad was a good thing, you know." Irritated, Evie pushed ahead of Jake as they entered their room. "It means he's not a part of whatever is going on." She sat on the side of the bed and slipped her shoes off.

"I love dogs. I'd never kick one." Jake set the locks on the door. "I'm in a bad mood for a reason. If Brad's in the clear, and I'm not totally convinced about that, it also means we're back to square one. Meaning we have no idea who is after you. It was easier when we could focus in on Brad. At least we had some place to start."

"I suppose." She pulled her deep pink top off, rummaged in her suitcase for a pale green pajama set, and dressed, very aware of Jake settling at the table in the corner, watching her. His scent lingered in her mind, made her want. "Why don't you tell me what's really bugging you?"

"How did you feel, seeing him again?"

Evie's cheeks burned. "What do you mean?"

"Did you want to, I don't know. Spend the night with him? Don't rush; think about it for a minute." He stretched his legs out and crossed them at the ankles.

She stared at him, at the bright burn of his blue eyes boring into her. "Are you asking me if I want to fuck my ex-boyfriend who ran out on me when I was fifteen?" Jake was the only person she wanted to fuck. Didn't he know that?

He shifted uncomfortably. "Yes."

"You think my judgment is that bad. Wow." Her heart rate sped up as she grew angrier. She jumped up and went to her suitcase, struggled to keep her breathing even. Dumped everything out of the suitcase onto the bed and began refolding every piece of clothing she owned, except for the dresses, which already hung in the closet. Fury had her hands shaking. She would not cry or scream. She would not cry or scream. Damn it, she would not cry or scream.

She took a steadying breath. "You're ridiculous. I can't believe you asked me that. Do you think that I'm such a slut, that I would go from your bed to his at the blink of an eye?" She glared at him while holding three pairs of colorful G-string underwear. She remembered him taking a pair like them off her with his teeth and caught her breath.

His gaze focused on the sheer material. "No. Of course not."

"Because that was some pretty serious judging of me you just did," she continued, ignoring her rising arousal. She continued to fold the wispy pieces of lingerie and tucked them into the small side pocket of her suitcase. Unfortunately, every piece of silk now had Jake associated with it.

"You're angry." He pulled off his suit jacket and strode to the closet to hang it up.

"Wow, what powers of observation you have. Yes, I'm angry. Damn it, Jake." She concentrated hard on folding her clothes, setting the dirty ones on one side of the big suitcase and the clean ones, a small number at this point, on the other side.

Jake yanked at the tie around his neck. "We need to talk, Evie." He unknotted it and hung it up.

She erupted. "Talk? We are talking. You're talking about me wanting to boink some other guy while sitting in the room we share. Which has me seeing all sorts of shades of red. Vermillion, and scarlet, and alizarin crimson. Carnelian and cerise and carmine, just to toss out a few. Yeah, I took an art class, so what, and why are you laughing?"

She glared at him as he went back to the chair in the corner, chuckling and pinching the bridge of his nose.

His laughter trailed off, and he sat, leaned forward, his hands dangling between his knees. "You keep me off balance, Evie. I've never known anyone like you, and unless plans change, tomorrow night we're headed back to San Diego. Which means everything will be up in the air."

There was a new note in his voice, something she hadn't heard before. Her heart gave a funny little flutter and she carefully put her yoga pants into the suitcase before rounding the bed and sitting on the corner facing him, finally giving him her whole attention. "What do you mean?"

He undid the top button of his collar. "Your stalker, for one. We still don't know who that is."

"True. And?"

He rubbed the back of his neck. "I know you've got this amazing career in front of you, and I don't want to do anything to stop you from achieving your dreams. But here's the thing, see. I'm not ready to let you go."

Her heart smiled. Yes, he knew the words to say. But she didn't want to soften too easily. She looked down at her hands, resisted sticking a fingernail in her mouth for a quick chew. "So, what do you want to do?"

"You're making me work for this aren't you?" He took a breath. "I want to keep on seeing you when we get home. See how we get along, when we're not moving from hotel to hotel."

Her heart thudded. He wanted her. And oh man, did she want him. She held onto her poise, not wanting to be all yippee-skippy about it and possibly scare him. "Because hotel hopping is so glamorous," she said, arching one eyebrow. "Can you cook?"

"Yes. Well, I can grill, and I can make breakfasts. You know, pancakes and eggs and toast, things like that." He relaxed, sat back again. "Can you? Cook, I mean?"

She wrinkled her nose. "Yes. My skills at breakfast run to cold cereal and yogurt. So when we wake up together, you're doing breakfast." After, hopefully, he did her. More than once.

"Deal," he said. "By the way, while we're together, there isn't anyone else. I don't share."

She nodded. "I'm not good at sharing, either. So we're exclusive. But when do you think you'll be ready to let me go? I need to know. So I can make plans," she added vaguely. The last thing she wanted was him to believe she thought they'd be permanent. Not when he couldn't think that way.

He gazed at her steadily. "What if I told you I wasn't sure? Could you live like that?"

She studied her hands, wishing she were in the process of undressing him right now. But this conversation was far too important to mess up. "I don't know," she mused. "Conway wants to get me out on the road again as soon as possible. It sounded like Brad was gearing up for a tour, too, and he mentioned having me open for him." She shrugged. "So maybe we set the end date for this as the day I go back out on tour?"

She glanced up and got trapped in his gaze, his eyes a burning blue now. She shivered and her body came to aching life.

"If that's what you want," he said slowly. "I promise you I will never interfere with your career. I'm not a musician, and I don't speak the language. As long as you trust Conway to steer you straight, that's good enough for me."

"Conway was good enough for Mike," she reminded him.

"Yes. True. Do me a favor?" He stood, pulling the shirt out of his pants. He unbuttoned each cuff before starting on the buttons down the front.

She watched him avidly, waiting for the tee shirt to come off so she could look her fill of his well-muscled chest and abdomen. "Anything."

"Push your clothes and the suitcase off the bed."

She scrambled to do as he asked, on her hands and knees on the bed pushing her suitcase and clothes to the floor on the other side. Her heart pounded and her sex grew plump and wet. "Are we going to have makeup sex?"

"Yeah. Okay with you?"

"Oh yeah." She turned over and leaned on her elbows, watching as he unzipped his trousers and took them and his boxers down in one smooth movement. He was hard and ready for her, and as he stalked toward her, she eyed him appreciatively.

He returned the favor, looking at her as though she were his favorite flavor of candy. He dropped onto the bed, eased her toward him. He nuzzled her neck, inhaled her unique scent.

"How slow can we go?" He murmured the words against her throat before scraping his teeth there, gently, where her pulse beat. He lifted the silk that covered her body up and off, and passed a possessive hand across her tight nipples. Laid her back against the pillows.

Evie melted into the bedding as Jake took loving inventory of her body. Kisses pressed on the curve of her shoulder. The bend of her elbow. One hand on her belly, he explored her hips, her upper thighs, rolled her over onto her stomach to lick the sensitive skin at the back of her knees. Worked his way up to the slight curve of her ass. Nipped her there, and she jumped.

"Jake."

He kept up the slow torture, kisses, nips, light little strokes, licking along her spine until she thought she'd go crazy. Her nipples rubbed against the sheets and she wiggled her hips. "Please, Jake," she moaned.

"Don't move," he said, and she heard the side table drawer open and close. Then big hands lifted her by the hips, drawing her back so her body draped over her knees, her arms in front of her. She peeked over her shoulder and saw desire stamped on his face. He bent to her, kissed her deeply. Stroked the wetness between her legs.

Anticipation shook her and she closed her eyes. He lifted her hips and, with one smooth stroke, filled her completely.

"This is…you are…oh man," she said on a moan. His hands held her still as he moved slowly outward, then just as slowly surged back within her. She felt owned, possessed, in the best way possible. Letting all thoughts flow out of her head, she let sensation rule her.

Jake spread a hand across her back, smoothed down the curve of her ass as he filled her. So trusting. So open. So damn wet. He'd never been more seduced by a woman than this one. So mesmerized. Was it any wonder that he wasn't ready to say goodbye? He had until her next tour to convince her to make this relationship more permanent.

Her body clenched around his, urging him to move faster, but he held to his pace, determined to give her everything he could give.

She was different. Important. He'd crossed his own personal boundary lines because of her and now here he was, deep within her even as a new part of him came to life, unfurled inside him, making him shudder with longing. He welcomed that feeling, knew it for what it was.

Gratitude burned inside him.

He focused once again on the woman beneath him. Kept surging in slowly, withdrawing slowly, until she melted further into the bed. Until her limbs went boneless. Until her whimpers became moans of need, and he had an overwhelming desire to watch her face. To kiss her.

Carefully pulling out, he rolled her over. Settled belly to belly, he caged her with his elbows on either side, and brushed her tumbled curls. Those dark eyes opened and she smiled as he entered her again, tilted her hips to take all of him.

He kissed her then, with a need that went beyond the mere physical one beating through him. His body sped up as his control slipped and he kissed her neck, nipped down to suckle on her breast.

Jake took her breath away. Evie held his head as he suckled, wondering at the change in him. The dark intent in his eyes when he looked at her stirred too many emotions inside. He surged within her again and she cried out, her orgasm completely taking her by surprise. She tightened her legs around Jake's waist, grasped him with her muscles. Milked him until he bucked, her name on his lips.

They shimmered together, shaken by the intensity of what they'd just shared. Jake lifted from her and was back to her before she could move. He lifted the covers over them.

Evie had grown used to sleeping with him and now nuzzled into him, happy when his arm draped around her and rested on her ass. With him, she felt safe. Cared for. She hadn't told him, but she wasn't ready to let go of what they had, either.

Not yet. Luckily they had a few weeks before they would have to say goodbye.

CHAPTER FIFTEEN

The next day, Conway arranged for the Sportsman's Lodge to rent them a room where they could practice. They couldn't plug in, and they couldn't play too loud, but at least there was room for everyone and their instruments.

Jake stayed in a corner out of the way and watched. On the surface, Brad was the epitome of laid-back cool in well-worn jeans, cowboy boots, and a tee shirt, looking loose and casual. But Jake also listened—to what was said and what wasn't—and noticed what no one else seemed to. Something was seriously bugging Brad.

Conway took control soon after everyone else had arrived.

"I'm thinking we let the set go on as normal, and then Brad can come out just before your last two songs, Evie. What do you think?"

"We used to sing 'St. James Infirmary' together when we were younger," she said. "How about we rearrange the order, and sing that as the third from the last song?" She turned to Brad. "Are you ready to revisit Old Joe's Barroom?"

"Sure am. You can sing the first part, I'll be Old Joe McKennedy, and then we'll take it from there, changing who does harmony and who takes lead. Let's run through it." He picked up his Martin and slung the strap around his neck.

"I like the sound of that. I'm ready when you all are. Okay?" She nodded at Bear, who tapped out a rhythm on the table with his hands. The bass guitar picked up on it, and she sang the opening notes and grinned at Brad's dropped jaw. Yeah, she had a set of pipes on her now.

They played it through several times and finally decided to switch off who had what verse and who sang harmony. An hour passed as they talked and worked and sang.

Even though Jake kept an eye out for it, he saw nothing but friendliness pass between Evie and Brad. No little touches, no quick glances, nothing personal at all. It was all about the music.

Finally Conway called a break, and eyed them thoughtfully. "You all sound great together. She'll make a great opening act for you, if you were serious about that offer yesterday."

"Starting an east coast tour just a couple of weeks from today through November, taking a break, then we swing through the southern states from February to April. Hit the west coast June through August." His eyes brightened. "It would be fun," he said. "You and Carl should talk about it, Conway."

"Hm. I guess we should. Are we done here?" Conway glanced toward Evie.

She stretched her arms over her head. "I think so. I didn't sleep much last night, so I could use a nap."

"Big night," Brad agreed. "I've got some stuff to do, as well. Thank you, boys. I appreciate you working me in." Brad shook each man's hand as they filed out, waiting until Bear closed the door behind them before he let out a breath. "I need to talk to you all."

Jake lifted his head at Brad's tone of voice. The tension he'd noted earlier was back. "Something's bothering you," he said. "I thought so."

"Yeah." He turned to Evie. "I'm sorry I'm not the man you deserved. I'm sorry I didn't stand up for myself when I left, all those years ago. I should at least have stood up for you, and I didn't do that, either. I'm so sorry."

Evie swigged some bottled water and wiped her mouth with her wrist. "Apology accepted. You wouldn't be here if I hadn't already forgiven and forgotten. Why are you bringing it up now?"

"It's my brother." Brad stopped, stricken.

"Ted? You know, I keep forgetting about him." She chuckled and cast an uneasy look to Jake. "What's up with Ted?"

"He's why I left you. He said I'd do much better without you, that you were too young to travel with us, and you were better off with Joyce and Gary."

Jake watched as pain washed across Evie's face and then drained away.

"Yeah. Well, I ran away a week after you did. After I was sure you weren't coming back, I ran. And I ended up with Mike Harper."

Brad's confusion cleared. "I wondered how that had happened."

Jake, impatient, broke in. "Why are you talking about Ted now?"

"He wiped me clean. I have no money right now, because my brother, who was also my financial manager, cleaned me out and left me high and dry."

Conway put up a hand. "Wait a minute. He had access to all your accounts? Even the one Carl keeps for you?"

"No, I still have that one account. But Ted basically ruined me. He didn't pay my taxes the last five years, either. A notice from the IRS was in my P.O. Box here in town. It's a mess."

Evie had been thinking hard. "Why? I don't understand it."

"Ted never got over us being made wards of the state." He turned and spoke to Jake. "My parents were drug addicts. I'm sure Evie must have told you."

"No. She didn't. She's remarkably loyal. Has very little bad to say about anyone." He smiled warmly at her and she came over to sit beside him. Dropped a kiss on his cheek.

"Thanks."

"You're welcome."

Brad blinked a few times and then took a deep breath. "Ted ran my life for a long time. I don't know if you knew that, Evie, but the only thing I ever did that he hated was bringing you to live with us. We used to fight about you all the time."

"But why? I don't get it."

Jake cleared his throat. "I'm guessing it was a power issue. Am I right?"

"Yeah." Brad spread his hands wide. "Until you, I worshipped him. I listened to him, and I did everything he told me to do. After you came, Evie, a big part of his spell over me had been broken. I had you to take care of, to teach, to sing with and dream with. When you turned thirteen is when Ted starting trying to separate us."

"I remember. You wouldn't let me touch your guitar."

"He said it was our ticket out of there. If you touched it, you might break it. Accidentally. We couldn't risk it." He shook his head. "Sounds stupid now," he added with a sheepish look.

"So you think Ted is behind the persecution of Evie?" Jake thought about it. "When did you go into rehab? Six months ago, right?" As he continued to think, his blood ran cold with fear.

"Right. He fought it. I didn't realize until I was going through rehab, but Ted didn't want me sober, you see. He preferred me controllable." Anger and sadness twisted Brad's face. "I still can't quite wrap my mind around it."

Jake took Evie's hand in his, unhappy at where his thoughts had led. "That's about when the weird letters started arriving. Do you know where Ted is now?"

"No. I don't have a clue. We own a house together in Tennessee, so I assume he's there, but when I called, I didn't get any answer. I couldn't even leave voicemail. And he knew I was getting out of rehab this week. I had my counselor call him and tell him the news."

Evie cleared her throat. "Sorry to take this conversation down a different path, but Brad, why would Ted call me a plagiarist? Do you have any clue?"

"He wrote a couple of my first songs. Changed things up just a bit, and it took me a long time before I realized they were your songs. I thought, wow, he'd heard you sing and remembered the lyrics. I was amazed, and thought that in a way we were keeping you with us. I didn't know he had your notebook, Evie, I swear. Not until last night, when Jake here told me his investigations had me on the skids. And then you asked about the book. Evie, the lyrics to 'Lullaby' are mostly yours, not Ted's." He sent her a pleading look. "I'm sorry I was too dense to notice."

"So Ted must have been behind Johnny M's interview, and not you. Do the two of you sound alike?" Jake shrugged. "If you do, or if you'd never had an interview with Johnny M before, that would be a perfect scam."

Brad turned to Jake. "I know what you mean. And no, I've never even met The Beast of Social Media. I don't like his style."

Evie spoke up then. "I have one more question."

Jake could feel the tension in Evie's body. He shifted, put his arm around her. She grabbed his other hand, but didn't look at him. He could tell that all her focus was on the man seated across from them.

Brad nodded. "Sure. Ask away. I don't want there to be any secrets between us, Evie. Not anymore."

"Did you ever try to find me that first year?"

He stilled, and sorrow came into his eyes. The moment stretched out until he finally shook his head. "I'm sorry. Ted—no. I didn't."

Jake watched as Evie drew in a deep breath before leaning into the warmth of his body. He rubbed his cheek on the top of her head and stared at Brad.

"Thanks. Then I made the right decision, leaving soon after you did. If I'd waited, if I'd stayed, my life would look very different right now." She turned to Jake, kissed him. "And I like my life just the way it is."

He smiled into her changeable eyes, and for a moment no one else was in the room.

Conway coughed, brought them back to the present. "Okay, so we know Ted is out there and needs a one-way ticket to the loony bin."

As Evie and Brad protested, Jake privately agreed.

Conway snorted. "Well, the loony bin or jail, you tell me. Have you spoken with Carl about the financial stuff?"

"Yeah. The wheels of justice have been put in motion." Brad stood, swaying a bit. "I'm going to my room."

"You checked in here?"

He turned to Jake. "It seemed easier. Assuming I can get a ride with you to the Topaz Room and back?"

Jake and Evie shared a look. "We'd actually planned on driving back to San Diego tonight, since it's such an early night," Evie said.

"I'll extend our stay another night," Conway said. "It's no bother, and we can afford it. As long as you two don't mind," he added.

"I'm good. But you'd better ask the others." Evie sent a sympathetic look to Brad. "Everything will work out."

He gave her a lopsided smile. "You always were such an optimist."

"Of course," she said in a light tone. "I had a knight in shining armor rescue me when I was very young. It's hard for me not to look on the bright side."

"Okay kids, let's break it up. We're about running out of time on this room. You sounded great together, by the way. I'm really looking forward to tonight's show." Conway stood, stretched, and ambled to the door. "I have client meetings all afternoon, so I'll meet you at the venue. Don't be late," he warned.

"Never happen. Thanks Con." Evie blew him a kiss.

"Coming, Brad?"

"Yes. I want to talk to you, Con." He picked up his guitar case and sketched a salute to Evie and Jake, still twined together. "Looks like you did good, Shortie."

"See you later, Bradley."

He grinned, and the two men were gone.

Evie wiggled and Jake moved so she could stand. She went to her guitar and wiped the strings down before putting it into its case.

"What a sad story. The one person you think would take care of you, to use you like that."

"It is sad. And scary, too. If he can do that to his own brother, what will he do to other people?" Jake had been going to say "you" but thought better of it. It chilled him to realize how, all unwittingly and so very long ago, Evie had come between two brothers. If they had both been normal, it wouldn't matter so much.

But from what little he'd heard, Ted hadn't been normal.

"What was your impression of Ted? Back when you lived with them, I mean."

Evie chewed on her left thumbnail as she thought. "He ruled Brad. He was older, though, so Brad and I had a similar schedule, and the three of us didn't hang together much on weekdays. When we did, Ted was in charge and I was the outsider. We got along about as well as siblings who aren't from the same family do, I guess." She wrinkled her nose. "None of that helps."

Jake stood then, coming over to her to wrap her up in a hug. "Yes, it does. I'm not sure how, exactly, but at least I can call the San Diego and the Las Vegas Police Departments and fill them in on what I know." He felt her stiffen in his arms. He pulled away so he could see her face, and brushed her tumbled curls back from her face. "Hey there. They may call me cracked, but it's the only lead we've got."

"I know. It doesn't make me feel any better, though. I just wish I had put more of an effort in getting to know him back then." She patted his chest. "But I guess everything had to happen the way it did, or we wouldn't be here right now, together."

Jake thought back along his own twisty life path, and for the first time knew he could finally make peace with his father's death. "You know, I'd like you to meet my mom when we get back home." He hefted her guitar and wrapped an arm around her waist.

She gave a little skip of joy. "Do I get to see your apartment, too?"

He laughed. "Such as it is. And we'll go running through Balboa Park."

"I haven't been to the Arboretum in years. Can we go there?"

"Absolutely. In the meantime, let's find some lunch and then a nap."

"I do like the way you think, Mr. Wells."

They headed to their room, both aware that underneath their patter, a sense of dread mounted between them like a ticking clock, counting down the minutes until Ted showed himself.

***

Their lovemaking that afternoon was long and slow and sweet. When Jake finally left her side, Evie lay slumped in the bed in a sensual stupor. She knew Jake wasn't happy about their plan for tonight, but it was their best shot. Forcing Ted's hand sooner rather than later meant she could get on with her life without the constant worry that he was out there, somewhere.

Jake came back to bed and curled around her. Evie sent him a quick smile before sighing.

"What's wrong?"

She twined her hand with his. The room was cool and dark, the drapes drawn against the hot summer sunshine. "This whole week has been magical." More than she had ever expected.

"Good magical? Or bad magical?"

"Overall, good. Definitely. But now I'm…I don't know. I feel like, hell…I don't know." Like they only had minutes left of their time together; like something terrible waited in the wings; like life as they knew it was going to end soon.

Jake shifted, taking her in his arms, and she cozied up to him, glad he was with her. "Everything will work out, Evie. I'll keep you safe, and everything will work itself out."

"I know. I just…there's something. Oh, I can't explain it. You probably think I'm being stupid."

Before she knew what was what, Jake sat up, pulled her to a sitting position and was shaking her gently by the shoulders.

"You've got to stop it, Evie. You're not stupid. You're not a child. You're an intelligent, beautiful young woman with a career ahead of you that you've worked very hard for. Stop denigrating yourself just because you're not almost forty, and I am."

Evie stared at him. Caught her breath on a hiccuping laugh. "Oh my God. I have been, haven't I? Damn."

"I told you that once before, if you remember," he said, and gentled his hold on her.

"You did. You know, Mike was something else."

Jake scooted back to lean against the pillows. "In what way?"

She faced him, dragged a pillow into her lap. "Well, at first I didn't want to go to school. I figured, why bother? But then he'd needle me, and I'd get fired up with the urge to prove to him I was smart. He finally bullied me into getting an AA in business, for which I now thank him. But the way he got me there was to point out my youth and naïveté and, well, lack of knowledge."

"Ah. So now you automatically think any older man is going to look on you as young and stupid?"

"When you put it that way, it sounds, well. Stupid. And young." She studied him, looking at the streak of silver in his hair, at his strong cheekbones and kind eyes. "I still have a lot of growing up to do," she said.

"Does one ever stop growing up? I don't think so. I have a lot to learn, as well. For instance, I have no idea what a fret is on a guitar."

She laughed. "Do you really want to know?"

"Yeah."

"I could teach you to play. For fun. You might like it."

He smiled at her. "I think I'll pass on the lessons. Maybe later." He checked the clock and beckoned. "Come and nap with me."

Evie snuggled up against him again and he pulled the covers up over them.

"Do you still miss the ocean?"

Surprised by the sudden subject change, Evie considered his question. "I did," she said. "Especially in the desert. But I haven't thought about it recently. Weird."

"Not so weird. At least it's only a two-hour drive to home from here. We'll be back in time for sunset tomorrow."

"Yeah." But the need for sleep had drifted away. Now all Evie could think about was tomorrow, and what their relationship would look like once they were home.

CHAPTER SIXTEEN

"You go on in. I want to talk to security," Jake said. They'd just pulled up to the Topaz Room parking lot. Jake shut her door and handed Evie her makeup case, and the driver of the town car pulled away. The band had come earlier to handle most of the setup.

She reached up and kissed him. "Don't take long," she warned, "or I'll send Conway out after you."

Jake had a bad feeling about tonight and enough experience not to ignore it. He watched until she vanished through the staff entrance at the side of the building. Stepping back, he made mental note of the entrances he could see. A three-story building, it gleamed golden in the setting sun. Small windows on the first couple of floors and big windows on the top floor. Walking the perimeter, he took note of the fire escape, the doors, which ones were obviously alarmed and which weren't. A useless exercise, most likely, but better to know than not know.

"Can I help you?"

Jake froze. Turned around. And stared in disbelief at the beautiful woman dressed in a black power suit with a very short skirt. His ex-wife. "Marisa? What the hell are you doing here?" Stunned, all he could think of was that she hadn't changed.

"Jake?" Chagrin crossed her lovely face. "I work here. Head of security. What are you doing here?"

He hadn't seen nor heard of her since their divorce and her subsequent dismissal from the force. He'd have been happier if he'd never seen her again, but that train had left the station. Narrowing his gaze, he scrutinized her. There were worry lines around her eyes and a definite downward droop to her mouth. Her hair was still being professionally done, as she'd been getting silver strands amongst the black since she was fresh out of school. "If you're head of security, then we're in trouble. I'm with Evie and Brad Gaines."

"I had heard about the problems. Con filled me in last night, though he didn't give me your name. You don't have anything to worry about," she said. She crossed her arms the way she did when annoyed. "We've got it covered. Your little singer won't be in any danger from her stalker." Her contemptuous tone pissed him off, just as it always had.

"You will leave Evie alone. If I find you even looking cross-eyed at her, I'll kick your ass to San Diego and back." Protective anger vibrated through him. "Stay away from her if you know what's good for you."

Marisa smirked at him. "Well. Took another one under your wing, did you? You have enough sisters. Or did you adopt this one? Playing daddy in your old age?"

An icy calm dropped over Jake. "Think what you like. You've been warned. Tell me. What kind of security do you have here? Metal detectors? Do you search bags at the door? Anything?"

"No one's died here, if that's what you're asking," she hedged.

"Which means you've got shit in the way of security. Great." Disgusted, he pulled out his cell.

"Who are you calling?" Was that anxiety in her voice?

He speared her with a hard glare. "A captain I know in the Hollywood Division. Hopefully he'll be able to send a few officers around."

"You can't just come in here and take over," Marisa protested. "This is my world, and I've got it taken care of. Nothing is going to happen, Jake. You're being ridiculous."

"Don't expect me to trust you. Just don't." He turned back to his phone. "Yeah, Gary, it's Jake Wells. Give me a call, buddy. I need some extra men at the Topaz Room tonight. I'm expecting trouble of the deadly kind." He ended the call and put the phone back into his pocket. "Walk the perimeter with me."

She hesitated. "There's nothing to see."

He shot her a cool look. "This is business. Walking the perimeter with me is part of your job."

Marisa flushed and tossed her black hair over her shoulder. "In that case, let's go." She spun on her heel and walked rapidly toward the front of the building.

Jake rubbed a hand over his forearm as he followed. Evie's name wasn't tattooed there, but it might as well have been.

***

Conway took Evie's makeup case and garment bag out of her hands the minute he saw the band, along with Brad, come through the back door into the club. "They're sold out, specifically for the eight-thirty show. The manager said they never pre-sell out, and never for the eight-thirty." He talked so fast his words were tumbling over themselves as he led them to the green room. "Plus, you guys get your own green room. The other bands are in another room. Your dressing room is in this corner, Evie." He disappeared through a door and came back out without the bags.

"No way. Seriously?" She grinned at Brad. "See what you did?" She looked around. Comfortable couches lined the walls, and there were two tables, one with food on it and one with drinks. Soda and bottled water and bottles of wine. She headed for the water, pleased when Jimmy, Reid, and Bear hunkered down at one of the couches. One of them pulled out a deck of cards.

"Hey, Evie. Wanna play poker?" Bear waved the deck.

"You'd clean me out," she declared. "Better not, but thanks anyway."

Brad reached out to shake Conway's hand. "Thank you for setting this up. I really appreciate it."

"All for a good cause. If we can clear Evie's name, we'll all sleep better," he said. "Where's Jake?"

Evie laughed. "He's searching out the security team. He'll be here soon. Gosh, I hope I'm ready for this." The other shows had been nerve-wracking, but this, after all, was Los Angeles. Not a place to fail.

"You're ready. Let's just run through it one more time. Evie will do her set, up until the last three songs. She'll go off stage to change, and the band will go off, too, take a break. Brad, you'll come on, sing 'Lullaby,' which is one of the songs based on her writing, and then Evie will come back out. The two of you will talk about old times. Evie will sing either 'Soul Savior' or 'Hold On', and then the band comes back out, the two of you will sing 'St. James Infirmary.' Afterwards, we should expect a bit of a stampede in the green room."

Evie plucked a bottle of water from a tub filled with ice. "As long as Jake is around, I'll be fine." She shot a quick look to Brad. "Any word from Ted?"

"Not one." He shifted uneasily. "His cell goes straight to voicemail."

"Are you worried?"

"Not sure what to think."

She patted his shoulder and passed him a bottle of water. "It'll all work out. I have to believe that, you know? It's what keeps me going, that belief."

"You always look on the bright side. It's one of the things I admire most about you."

The door opened and Jake came in. Evie shivered at his set face. "Is everything okay?" Jake wasn't alone. A tall brunette followed him in. Her body screamed sex, the short black skirt and the black jacket hugging centerfold curves. Evie saw the bulge under her jacket and was reassured. Security. All was well.

"Hi. How's the security here? And do you want some water?" She held out a bottle to Jake.

"Security here sucks, but I'm getting it handled. Evie, this is Marisa Campbell. Marisa, Evie Marcherand."

Evie's eyebrows rose and she turned toward Jake, dismissing the other woman. There could only be one Marisa who would put that closed look on Jake's face. "Hey. Wanna find a closet and go make out before the show starts?"

Marisa huffed. "It's not Campbell; it's Tarrington."

"You got someone else to marry you? Color me shocked." Jake's forehead dropped to Evie's as she looked up at him. "Don't worry, E. She's not important."

Evie put a hand on his cheek and guided his mouth to hers, kissing him passionately, grateful when he relaxed. They parted and Evie scanned his face. "I'm not worried, as long as you're okay."

He squeezed her waist and kissed the top of her head. "I swear. I'm fine. Like I said, security here sucks, but we'll be fine."

"Randall Blue, the owner, assured me everything would be in place. This is not an issue you want to mess with," Conway said, pointing a finger at Marisa. "The contract we signed assured everyone's safety. If that gets screwed up, you can expect a lawsuit."

Brad took charge smoothly. "I'm sure we don't need to fling around words like lawsuit. Nothing's happened. Now, Marisa, why don't you give me a tour of the place? I'll be able to look at the security issue through impartial eyes."

"That's an excellent idea, Mr. Gaines."

Before the rest of them knew what was happening, Brad and Marisa left.

Evie felt all the tension leave Jake. "That must have been a shock," she said.

"You have no idea. If I weren't working, I'd slug down some whiskey."

Evie giggled.

"When do you start getting ready?" He ran his hand through her curls.

She tilted her head, enjoying the feel of his fingers there, and focused on his question. "Um. In about ten minutes. It'll take me about half an hour, and then there'll be five or ten minutes left before we go on. Why?"

"Take a walk with me." He took her hand and tugged. Willingly, she followed as he led her out of the room and into the corridor. No one was there except the two of them. Faintly, the first band of the night could be heard, playing above them.

They stood there, neither of them speaking. Evie watched all the emotions swirling around in Jake's eyes but couldn't tell what, exactly, he was feeling. "What is it? Is something wrong?"

He leaned against the wall with a sigh and reached for her hand. "No. Not really. I just have a bad feeling about this, and I don't know how to fix it. I don't suppose you're willing to cancel?"

"Because of Marisa?" At his nod, she gave it some thought before answering. "No. They sold out because of us. I'm not going to cancel because your ex is running security, or because you have a funny feeling about the performance. You said you have help coming, right?"

"Gary's a buddy of mine in the PD up here. I left him a message and he rang me back. He can spare two men and a patrol car and will keep the rest of the squad on alert."

"That's great. Right?" But he didn't seem happy about it. Evie rubbed her hand down his arm. "You're doing due diligence. Marisa is very pretty. You hadn't mentioned it."

Jake shook his head. "She's always been that way. A hothouse flower with staying power. That's what I used to call her."

"Ah." Unreasonable hurt gathered like a knot in her chest. "She's wearing a gun."

"I know. She's a good shot. I'm not worried about her."

Evie looked up at him, but his eyes were unrevealing. "What are you worried about, then?"

He sighed and pulled her close. "I worry. It's a habit. So, can I be on stage with you?"

Her voice sharpened. "Nothing is going to happen. We're going out there, we're going to take Los Angeles to pieces, and we're going to be a hit."

He kissed her neck. "And then we're going back to the hotel and having some hot hotel sex. And champagne."

"If we had time, I'd say let's find a bathroom with a door that locked, and have a quickie," she muttered against his lips. She slipped her arms around his waist and stopped, shocked, when her hand touched hardware. "You're wearing a gun?"

"I have a concealed weapons permit. Ex-cop, remember?" He wrapped her in his arms. "Wait. It's okay for Marisa to wear a gun, and not okay for me to do the same?"

"This is Los Angeles." She shrugged. "And it's the first time I've met her. But you wearing a gun tells me that you're really worried." She moved her hand away from his shoulder holster. "Now you're making me really worried. You know what they say about guns. It's hard to get off a shot if you're not carrying one. Which means *you* expect there might be the possibility of shooting tonight."

"I'd rather have the gun and not need it than need it and not have it." He smoothed a strand of hair off her face. "This is all I can do. I don't think it's enough, but it's all I've got. Marisa has two guys working with her here. They know, as do the local cops. Conway knows, and Randall Blue, the owner, knows. It wouldn't surprise me if a few more guys around here were carrying concealed."

"With permits?" She tried to make it a joke, but neither one of them laughed. "You're not going to need it."

"I hope not."

She sighed. "It was more fun talking about having a quickie."

"You're the one who said we didn't have time." He gave her another hard kiss before he stepped back. "I'm going to hold you to the sex and champagne, later."

"Good." She slipped her hand into his. "I swear, everything is going to be fine, and you're not going to need that piece of hardware strapped to your underarm." She tugged and they went back into the green room.

The boys were hooting in the corner.

"No way. Four aces? Damn, just when four ladies don't matter," muttered Jimmy. "Stupid cards."

Reid raked in the pot. Evie went to them, wanting a little uncomplicated downtime. Maybe they could deal her in.

"You're playing with twenties?" She stood there, surveying the table between them, hands on her hips.

"Yeah. We didn't have any change, and no chips, and we didn't want to use potato chips," Bear said.

"That's an expensive buy-in."

Bear shrugged.

"I'm out. That was all the money I had." Jimmy leaned back.

Reid gave them each their twenties back. "Let's just play blackjack, and not bet. Okay?"

"Evie, time to get dressed." Conway looked up from his phone, where he was checking email.

"Got it." With relief, she left them all behind. Finally, something she could do with the butterflies in her stomach.

The dressing room consisted of a long counter, backed by a mirror surrounded with bright, unflattering lights. A vase of red roses sat there, next to a smaller vase of cheerful sunflowers. Her garment bag hung on a short clothes rack against the back wall. A big improvement over the closet that had been the dressing room at the Four Parrots in Las Vegas, that's for sure.

Feeling giddy, she checked the cards that came with the flowers. Conway had sent the roses, which was too sweet. To her surprise, the sunflowers were from Brad. Huh. Maybe he'd learned a thing or two the past ten years.

She stripped off her clothes and put on her show robe, a slinky number in cream silk. She proceeded to apply spray foundation, set it with a mineral powder, and she added false eyelashes, mascara, thick eyeliner, smoky shadow. A slight darkening of her eyebrows and a deep cherry-red lipstick, a faint brush of blush, and twenty minutes later her face was done.

A knock sounded and the door opened. Marisa came in and shut the door behind her.

Evie's pulse kicked into high gear. She turned, leaned against the counter. "What do you want?" Marisa had turned and was surveying the room, her perfume thick and heavy. Poison. Evie wrinkled her nose. She'd never been sure whether she liked the designer scent or not. Still wasn't sure. She waited for Marisa to say something. Her gaze flicked over the flowers in the corner before coming to rest on Evie. She raised an eyebrow. "Well?"

"You're so young."

"Excuse me?"

Marisa crossed her arms. "I made a mistake when I let Jake go."

Anger blinded Evie for a moment, stole her breath. She blinked. "Excuse me. When did you let him go? Before, or after you lied about how he treated you?"

Marisa's eyes widened. "Not everything is as he told you."

Evie's hands closed into fists. "How do you know what he told me? No. Never mind. I don't want this conversation. You need to leave, and right now. I don't care that you have a gun and could shoot me. Just get the hell out of my dressing room, and stay out of my sight, or I will deck you."

Marisa shook her head in pity. "Poor thing. Too small to be of much use, and far too young for a man like Jake. He's finding your youth a novelty, I'm sure, but his life revolves around his work. Don't for a minute think you'll be able to keep his interest when better women than you have failed."

"You? You are not a better woman." Evie grabbed the big can of hairspray and pointed it accusingly at Marisa. "Get. Out. Right. Now." She took a step toward Marisa, her voice escalating in volume with each word.

Marisa's eyes widened. She turned and left without another word.

Evie locked the door behind her and sat in her chair, trembling with anger. She stared at herself in the mirror. A part of her believed Marisa, that Jake was just enjoying her. A novelty, like Marisa had said.

Jake may have said he wanted to continue it, but wouldn't it be better for them to stop it right away, rather than prolong their parting? It would hurt, yes, but it would hurt a lot less to do it quickly.

A knock came at the door. "Five minutes to places, Evie. Five minutes." It was Conway.

"Thank you, five minutes." Enough wallowing. She had a show to do. Evie stood and went to the mirror.

She'd already worked on her hair back at the hotel, so all she had to do now was slip on the red dress and her heels, and she'd be good to go.

Looking at the final results in the mirror, she rubbed her arms against the chill of the air conditioning. Her stomach clenched and she forced down the rising nausea. She would not be sick. Instead, she focused on the powerful feeling of performing in front of an audience, of moving them, and her nausea subsided. She breathed easier.

Yes, this was an important night. But if she were going to be a performer, *every* performance would be important. Pleasing the audience was her number one job, and it didn't include being sick before singing. That was a cliché she could easily do without. Right?

Giving herself one last glance in the mirror, she winked at her reflection. "Time to knock 'em dead," she said, and gave herself a thumbs up.

***

Jake stood at the back of the standing-room-only crowd rocking out to Evie's performance. There was a good buzz going, and he saw plenty of photos being taken with cell phones. In spite of the good vibe, his danger radar was still going off and it drove him nuts.

The room could hold a maximum of five hundred people. He estimated the maximum had been exceeded by close to fifty, which made moving through the crowd difficult for the waitresses. The air conditioning couldn't handle the crowd and the room had grown stuffy with the scent of perfume and beer and too many bodies pressed too close together.

Evie's song came to a close and the applause was enthusiastic, with some hooting and hollering. Her second set was over. Now she'd be introducing Brad.

Jake kept scanning the crowd for trouble. Saw Marisa doing the same on the opposite side of the room. She looked tense, and Jake wondered if something had happened. His senses went on high alert.

"Thank you, everyone. You're a terrific audience, you know that? Thank you so much." Evie's whiskey-honey voice filled the room. "We've got a treat for you tonight. This is the first time I've ever introduced him, but I hope it won't be the last. Ladies and gentlemen, I want you to give a big welcome to one of my best friends from a long time ago, the boy who frightened off the bullies and washed my scraped knees. Bradley Gaines!"

Brad strode out onstage carrying his guitar, and the audience surged to their feet, cheering and whistling and applauding.

Jake had to admit they looked good together on stage. Evie was in the blue dress, and Brad wore jeans, cowboy boots, a plaid flannel shirt, and a cowboy hat. City sophistication meets country boy.

"Thank you, Evie."

She blew him a kiss and went offstage to change.

Brad settled in front of the microphone and started strumming. "Now, there's some stuff going around about my good friend Evie that just isn't true. Anybody out there who wants to record this with your cell phone and put it up on YouTube, well, you've got my permission."

Phones immediately rose in the air. He chuckled. "Okay then. So, I'm going to play you one of my most favorite songs in the world. It's also my first number one hit, from way back when. It's called 'Lullaby,' and to be honest, Evie wrote ninety percent of the lyrics and not my brother Ted, like I had originally thought. So I'm setting the record straight. Evie, this Lullaby's for you."

He sang the simple, sweet song of a man singing his children to sleep and telling them their mama was a soldier and would be home soon.

Jake hadn't heard it in years, but after listening to her songs this past week, he could tell that Evie had written it. The depth of emotion that threaded every one of her songs was clearly there. As the song finished, the crowd cheered and applauded.

When Evie reappeared, dressed now in jeans and tennis shoes and a pink plaid shirt, the audience went wild.

Brad put his hands together and bowed slightly in her direction. Evie blushed and punched him in the arm, and the audience laughed. Jake relaxed. The chemistry between them was there, it was real, and the audience could see it. He could just imagine the tweets being sent out.

"Thank you so much for bringing that song to the world, Bradley. Not sure if it would ever have happened without you and Ted."

"I'm just sorry he took your song without either of us knowing about it." His sincerity rang true.

Jake frowned. Scanned the crowd again. Marisa had bent her head to talk to one of the patrons. She didn't say much before she moved off. Jake shifted his location but couldn't easily tell who she'd been talking to.

"Water under the bridge, my friend," Evie said. "Ready to sing 'St. James Infirmary'?"

Brad tipped his hat to her. "Just like old times. Ready when you are."

"Let's go, then." She strummed the opening chords of the song. Brad adjusted the standing microphone.

The sound of gunshots came out of nowhere, a spray of bullets hitting the light fixtures scattered across the ceiling. Jake pulled his weapon.

Brad jumped in front of Evie, took her down to the ground as glass rained down onto the small stage and out into the audience. The room erupted in screams and people everywhere dropped to the floor and ducked under tables. People at the back of the room sprinted for the exits.

"Jake!"

"Evie!" Jake's heart hammered at the panic in Evie's voice as he scanned the room, and prayed she'd stay still and quiet and let Brad protect her.

A sandy-haired man stood in the aisle on the right side of the room, fifty feet in front of Jake, holding an AR15 and looking like he knew how to use it. Jake swore under his breath. How did he get that monster in the room? Bloody stupid bouncers. And he'd bet his last dollar this was the missing Ted.

"Nobody move, and nobody will get hurt," the man called out. The room stilled, the silence broken only by a woman's soft sobbing.

"Give it up, Ted," Jake called from behind him, hoping to draw his attention.

Ted didn't turn around. "Shut up. The only person I want to talk to is Evie."

Brad sat up, keeping his body between Evie and his brother. "Ted, stop. Right now. So you stole a couple of Evie's songs. So what? Like she said, water under the bridge. Put the gun down and walk away before you do something really stupid."

"Now you're blaming her songs on me? Do you think I'm stupid, to take the fall for you? I'm the one who dragged you out of pathetic El Cajon, and away from that stupid girl. I'm the one who brought you to Vegas, who introduced you to the people who made you into a star," Ted pointed out. "You stole that notebook of Evie's, not me. Never me."

His voice was even. Far too calm, indicating to Jake he had a plan. Fear for Evie's safety slicked Jake's stomach. He didn't want to shoot to kill. From what he'd seen, Ted hadn't actually hurt anyone as yet.

The security guard on the opposite side of the room from Ted was talking quietly into his earwig. Jake fervently hoped he was relaying information to police who were on their way. But in the meantime, there were all these people. Please God, let this not turn into another massacre. There had been too many of them lately.

Quickly and silently, Jake urged the people nearest him to get up and move to the exit. A waitress noticed what he was doing, and urged the people near her to get up and get out. Slowly, quietly, people farthest from the stage and farthest from the shooter left the room.

Ted hadn't finished with his rant. "You wanted to bring her with us. She was fifteen, you ass. We both would have gone to jail if we'd taken her, too. You know that."

"I know that's what you told me," Brad said. "Yeah, you gave me a push out of the gate, true. But you stole to do it. You stole from our foster parents. You stole from where you worked. You liked it when I developed a taste for whiskey and cocaine, because you could control me. Well, it's over, Ted. So put the damned gun down and just leave. These people haven't done anything to you."

Jake had been taking small steps to the right, to get closer to Ted. Marisa, too, was edging toward him. People moved out of the way so he could pass, all of them as quiet as possible. All he had to do was get the gun from Ted, and it would be over.

"It's all about Evie," Ted snarled. "You've been in love with Evie since she was six. Do you have any idea how pathetic that is?"

"She made me realize the world isn't such a bad place," Brad said. "You hated the world and everyone in it since Mom and Dad left us. Evie showed me a better way of looking at life. Of course I'm going to be drawn to that. Who wouldn't be?"

"You imbecile. We could have sued her if you'd just kept pouring the whiskey down your throat."

"How many other writers did you steal from, Ted?"

"Shut up."

"Come on, tell me. Tell everyone in here how many people over the years that you've screwed out of royalties. Out of a career." Brad had scooted a bit toward the front of the stage, still keeping between Evie and Ted.

"Don't put your shortcomings on my head, Brad. And stop moving, you idiot."

"You even stole from me when I went into rehab. You stole all my money." Brad's voice had an ugly edge to it.

"Shut up. Shut up. Shut up."

"Ted, drop it." Marisa's voice.

Jake, horror stricken, started forward but knew he'd never get there in time.

Ted turned and shot at Marisa, who was standing a mere five feet behind him, at the same time she shot him. He got off two shots and Marisa went down.

What was left of the crowd gasped.

"Nobody move," Ted shouted, panting. Marisa's shot had hit him in the right shoulder.

Before Ted's gaze swept the rest of the crowd, Jake dropped to all fours, his heart going like a jackhammer. She hadn't been shooting to kill. He was pretty sure Ted had. He couldn't tell where she'd been hit. To his surprise, tears gathered in his throat for the woman who had once been his wife.

"Now, where were we?"

Jake peered up to where Ted stood, facing the stage once more. He needed to angle further out of Ted's line of vision and keep low. He mentally urged the cops to hurry.

He'd have one chance at this. If he screwed up, it was likely that more people would die, and he really didn't want anyone dying on his watch. There were people on the floor in front of Ted, and Jake wondered how long he'd sat in the audience, waiting for his chance.

Evie spoke up from behind Brad. Her smoky-sweet voice, the one that had gutted him the first time he'd heard it, rang out. Jake froze with fear.

"Ted, would your mother approve of you right now?"

CHAPTER SEVENTEEN

For a moment no one moved or breathed, it seemed. Then Ted lifted the gun toward her. "What did you say?"

"Stay down," Brad said in a low voice.

"Shut up, Brad." She moved so Ted could see her. "I said, would your mother approve of you now?" She could see him, standing there with people all crouched below him, like a tyrannical god lording it over mere mortals. But the tyrant was unstable, and one shoulder was covered in blood. A couple of dark shapes were moving toward him. She kept her gaze on Ted, though, not wanting him to get distracted. She said a quick prayer for Jake's safety.

"Leave my mother alone."

Evie kept her voice as calm as possible. "I wrote 'Lullaby' for you, you know. I understand that's why you thought it was yours. I truly believe that your mother wanted to stay and take care of you, but the courts took you away from her, and then she died of a broken heart. Isn't that what you told me?"

"Evie, you were just eight or so when I told you that. How can you remember?" The gun in Ted's hand drooped slightly, and he took a step forward. There was something in his face that made her think she was reaching him.

"You were sitting on the back step of the restaurant, in tears, missing your mom and afraid to let Brad see you like that because you had to keep it together for him. He worshipped you, and you only had him to love. Of course I remember."

Ted sniffed, and his voice came out on a tremble. "You wrote 'Lullaby' for me? No one has done anything like that for me. Ever."

Someone whimpered in the audience. To keep Ted's attention, she talked louder. "I'd been without my mom for a long time, too. So I guess I wrote it for both of us. Do you think you could put the gun down now? You're bleeding. You need a doctor."

The minute she said the words, she knew she'd made an error. Gone was the soft, remembering Ted. He snarled and raised the barrel of the gun.

"Not going back to a hospital. Thanks, though, for that little trip down memory lane. Bringing up memories I'd much rather not ever think of again. You're the first to go."

He aimed and Brad pushed her against the ground again even as Ted yelled and bullets went spattering. Fire stung along her arm. Brad jerked, swore under his breath. "I'm sorry, Evie. Sorry."

Evie heard his words but was too scared to reply. Sounds of a scuffle, swearing, and then an unearthly howl went up. Evie waited breathlessly, her face smashed against the stage floor, her torso lying underneath Brad, her heart thudding hard.

"Got him."

She thought it was Jake's voice, but she couldn't be sure. Hope surged within her.

"Make way, folks. Make way. LAPD coming through."

"Nooo. That's my gun. I have my rights, man. You can't take that away from me. Second amendment, second amendment," Ted ranted.

"You don't have the right to hold hostages, buddy. Let's go."

"Brad, get off me. I think they got him. Brad." She turned slightly, saw that Brad's eyes were closed. Alarmed, she scooted out from underneath his limp body and noted the sticky wetness on the back of his shirt.

"Oh no. Oh Brad." She tore off her flannel shirt, ignoring a sting along her arm, and pushed it against his wound. "Jake. Brad was hit." She looked up then, saw Ted being taken away in handcuffs. The few people left in the club were slowly getting up off the floor, shaking glass out of their clothes. Some were crying and there was a lot of slugging back the alcohol still on whatever table happened to be near. She searched for Jake, knowing he had to be there in the house somewhere. There… "Jake?"

But Jake didn't hear her. She watched as he knelt over a still form in a black suit. "Come on, Marisa," he begged. "Hang in there. Be the tough bitch I know you are." He cradled her in his arms. Her face was pale and her eyes closed. "What's the ETA on the ambulances?"

"Three minutes," one of the cops on the scene called.

Evie's eyes blurred with tears. She caught her breath and looked down at the blood seeping from beneath her hands. *Come on, Brad.* A hand touching her shoulder made her gasp.

"Evie. Thank God you're okay." Conway knelt at her side. "What's up with Brad?

"He was hit. It's his back."

Conway grimaced. "I'll press down for you while you take off your tee shirt, add it to the flannel." He shrugged out of his jacket. "You can wear this."

"Come on, Brad." She pulled off her tee shirt, pressed it against the wound. She looked around, her panic building. "Where the hell are the paramedics?"

"Let me take over putting pressure, while you put on my jacket. You're something else, kid."

The pride in his eyes warmed her as she put on his jacket over her black lace bra, and rolled up the sleeves. The silk lining stung the back of her arm. "Hell." She pulled the jacket off her arm and twisted around to look at it.

A red streak, part burn, part blood, bisected her upper arm. "I got hit. Damn it."

Conway hissed. "As soon as the paramedics arrive, I'll send them over to you."

It felt like hours, but in truth they arrived within a couple of minutes. One asked her some brief questions, another stabilized Brad, put him on a gurney, and got him out of there, a cop following.

"Evie." Jake was there, hugging her. "I've got to go with Marisa." Anguish lined his face. She kissed him.

"Go."

He took a few steps away. "We still need to talk."

"Again?" She blew him a kiss. "Go. You know where I live."

Evie watched as Marisa was loaded onto another gurney and taken away, with Jake at her side. Another paramedic cleaned her up before he added a light bandage to her arm. He mentioned she might need a tetanus shot and should see her own doctor. She put Conway's jacket back on and fastened all three buttons as the paramedic went on to his next patient. The few audience members who were still in the house had bruises and cuts, but nothing major. People were talking and texting like crazy as the paramedics checked folks out.

Two policemen were working the room, talking to people and then letting them go. The chaos died down as the room slowly emptied. Pale waitresses were walking through the few people who were left, offering free coffee and wine. Most people stuck with coffee. She knew what she needed and wondered if there was any chance of getting a plate of French fries.

Bear came out onstage then, flanked by Reid and Jimmy. They rushed to her side. "You're okay, right?"

"I'm fine. Grateful you guys were still offstage." She hugged Bear, felt safe in his big embrace.

"We called the cops the minute the shooting started," Jimmy said. "Kept them on the line the entire time, though it turned out they'd already been called."

"Life with you sure is interesting," Reid said on a drawl. Jimmy chuckled in agreement and they both gave her quick hugs.

"You guys did good," she assured them.

"At least now there's no doubt who wrote 'Lullaby.' That was good of Brad. Didn't think he'd actually admit anything," Bear said. "Too bad about the brother."

Jimmy glanced around the busy room. "How much longer do you think it'll be?"

"Well, we haven't talked to the cops yet, so I'm guessing it'll be a while. I'd love a glass of wine," she said. "And if the kitchen wouldn't mind, some fries would be awesome."

"I'll bring a bottle from the green room." Jimmy dashed off.

Reid gave her a rare smile. "I'll go charm the kitchen staff."

"Come on, let's see if we can grab a booth and get comfortable. I'm willing to bet the rest of the night has been cancelled. Box office nightmare, that," Bear added.

It took less time than she expected. The band had been questioned and released, and Evie had just received her fries when the police came around to her.

"Miss Marcherand?"

"Hi." She smiled at the officer standing at her table.

"I'm Detective Davies. I just have a few questions."

"Go ahead. Want some fries?" She picked one up, chewed it.

"No, thanks. This won't take long. How do you know Ted and Brad Gaines?"

Evie sighed. So it begins, she thought, and steeled herself to answer all sorts of probing questions.

By the time they were done, she was wrung out.

"Thanks for your cooperation. I'm sure the DA will be in touch to take down your deposition." The detective shook her hand.

"You have my number." She watched him go with relief.

Conway came to her, the sleeves of his pink dress shirt rolled to the elbows. Blood stained one side of his shirt. "I've packed up your dressing room. Everything's in the car now."

She stared at him, shocked, barely listening to him. "Did you get shot?"

"What?" He looked down. "God, no." He brushed at the stains. "I was helping one of the ladies. She was kind of panicky. Glass cuts on her arms."

"Oh." Evie stood and swayed. "Can you take me home?"

"The car is waiting. We'll be at the hotel before you know it." He moved to put an arm around her, but she stopped him.

"No." Evie shut her eyes. She missed Jake with every cell of her body, but he was busy. He'd come to her when he could, but in the meantime, she just wanted to be home, in her cozy house. "I want to go home. To San Diego." She opened her eyes to see the speculation in Conway's, but he merely nodded. "I'll have Thelma Lou pack your things at the hotel and bring them down tomorrow, with the rest of the band. Come on, honey. Let's get you home."

She allowed him to put an arm around her. Even though the jacket had all three buttons done up, the deep vee left her pale skin exposed and she clutched it closed with one hand. Conway walked her through the club and out the front doors to the car waiting for them.

Camera flashes went off the minute they stepped outside. Paparazzi shouted questions, but neither Conway nor Evie said a word.

They made it into the limo with no one trying to stop them. Maybe it was because the cops were there, holding the door open and directing traffic. Evie didn't know, but gratitude filled her as the car moved smoothly into traffic. She leaned back against the leather seat and wondered how her heart could still beat, after all the heartbreak that night.

"Well, damn. We have to go back to the hotel after all. I still need to pack and get my car. I'll drive us."

Evie bit her lip. "Are you sure you feel up to it? I don't want to wear you out for nothing."

His kind eyes met hers. "You really need to be home, right? This isn't about Jake?"

"I'm tired. In shock. Way too emotional. I need home, everything that is familiar to me. Not another soulless hotel room in another city. Not right now." She certainly didn't want him to think she was running from Jake, because she wasn't. "Jake needs to be with Marisa tonight. I know that. I'm fine with that."

"Good. Because you two look good together. Like you fit, you know? You don't want to throw something like that under the bus without thinking it through."

She gave a brief laugh. "He knows where I live." Unbidden, doubt crawled through her. "At least, I hope he comes back."

"He will come back to you. You can count on it." Conway took her hand in his. "I don't want you to make my mistake, tossing away the best thing I'd ever known. I was stupid, and I've been paying the price ever since."

Evie raised her eyebrows. "Seriously? You are a serial dater. You were in love? Really in love?"

"Serial dater. Huh." Conway rubbed his face. "Yeah. Really in love. Hannah was the girl next door. We were the Joey and Dawson of our neighborhood, only without the intellectual film discussions and gorgeous water scenery."

"Joey and who?" Evie yawned.

"*Dawson's Creek*, the TV show? Never mind. Hannah and I were friends until high school, and then—we weren't friends. One night, her date didn't hear her say 'no.' I heard. He didn't bother her again." He rubbed his knuckles and grinned.

"You were her knight in shining armor." She could see it. "How romantic. Did she fall at your feet in gratitude?"

"She got pissed at me, said she could have handled it." Conway shrugged. "It's an old story. Sorry. It's late and I'm still wired and nowhere near drunk enough."

"And with a long drive in front of you before you can get drunk enough." She reached for his hand, held it. So grateful he was in her life. "You're a good man, Conway."

He looked scandalized. "For pity's sake, don't tell anyone. If word gets around that I'm not a complete nincompoop, I'll never be able to finagle amazing deals for my clients. I capitalize on my appearing stupid."

Evie smiled. "Your secret is safe with me." Hidden depths. Conway had lots of them, apparently, which made her like him even more. "It's too bad I can't fall in love with you. You're just about perfect."

"Except for the whole lack-of-chemistry thing." He rubbed her arm and smiled. "Mike made us family."

"Yeah. He did. He was good people." She yawned big.

"Go to sleep, Evie," he advised. "I'll make sure to wake you. We'll be on the road again within half an hour of hitting the hotel, on our way home."

She yawned again. "Can I stay in your room until it's time to leave?"

"Of course. Do you want me to leave a note for Jake?"

"No. He knows where to find me." She shifted closer to him and leaned her head against his shoulder. The rest of the way to the hotel her mind was filled with images of the past week. Jake in Las Vegas, Jake holding up baby clothes looking totally perplexed, Jake kissing her a bit desperately in the hallway of the club, just a few hours earlier.

Jake holding Marisa in his arms as she bled, and the anguish on his face. The hug he gave her, just before he followed Marisa to the hospital. No, she wouldn't leave a note. She wasn't sure what she could say that wouldn't sound wrong.

CHAPTER EIGHTEEN

A month later, Evie signed her name with a flourish on the last of three copies of the contract. She pushed them across to Conway and sat back, not sure how she felt about it. "There you go." The next step in her career. A five-month, forty-city tour, opening for The Band Perry.

"You won't regret it, Evie. The touring will be good for you." Conway set the papers to one side. "I should tell you that Lana Kirkland's interview is finally up on the *Las Vegas Weekly* blog."

"She left it kind of late, didn't she? That was all over a month ago." Evie gazed out the window. Heat had the buildings opposite them shimmering. It had been a long month since the tour. Since the shooting. Since she'd seen Jake.

"She got an exclusive from Brad, wanted to run them concurrently. And did I tell you that the first psych eval came back on Ted? He's tucked away in a private mental hospital until the trial."

"Poor Brad. He had always looked to Ted to take care of everything. I won't have to testify, will I? My deposition takes care of that, right?"

"I believe you're in the clear on that. But you know the wheels of justice crank slowly."

"Terrific. That's just damned peachy." She rubbed her eyes. "Sorry. I'm just tired." Tired of Brad, of Ted, of hearing gunshots in her sleep, of missing Jake. Tired of being alone.

"Still not sleeping?" Conway leaned forward on his desk. "Should I start worrying about you?"

"I've been thinking, and making notes. Maybe I should write a memoir about the whole thing. Brad and Ted and the foster family. Meeting up with Mike and my time with him. What do you think?" She met Conway's gaze and didn't flinch as he studied her.

"If that's something you want to do, I know I could sell it," he said slowly. "But only if you really want to do it. Thinking about writing while on the road?"

"It's something to do. Long days, you know." She shrugged. "Just don't tell anyone. I don't want to do anything about publishing it until I've got it finished. Just in case I can't write worth crap."

"Not a problem. So tell me, has he called you? Jake."

She picked at the cuticle on her pinkie finger. "We talk every couple of days. Marisa had to have major heart surgery. Of course Jake would be there, taking care of her. That's who he is. The guy who takes care of people." She shifted in her chair, sent a wry grin to Conway. "I'm considering buying a cell phone."

"You should have one. Glad Jake is making you consider it. What are you two going to do when he gets back?"

She shrugged. "We're friends. I'm going on tour, and he's going to Spain and France." At Conway's skeptical look, she flushed. "It's not like that with Jake and me. We were always a temporary sort of thing." Irritated, she pushed out of the chair and walked to the window. "A tour thing. Besides, he's so much older than me."

"Like that matters," he scoffed. "You can fool yourself, kiddo, but you can't fool me. I sat across from the two of you at dinner. I watched you both while we dealt with Brad. I saw the way your face lit up when Jake walked into the room. I witnessed his protective possessiveness where you were concerned."

"Exactly." She whirled around and pointed at Conway, her heart aching. "That's my point. He's spent years looking after people. His mother, his sisters, Marisa, me. Now he's back looking after Marisa. I'm just someone else for him to feel responsible for, that's all. I need better than that. I need more. Hell, Conway. I deserve more than that."

Conway stood and sighed. He came to her and hugged her. "You do deserve more than that. You deserve the very best that love has to offer. I just want you to make sure you know what you're doing. He's good for you. I think you're good for him. I think there's more there.

She kissed his cheek and stepped back. "Thanks for your concern, but I'll be fine. I'm a big girl. He said he would be home sometime today, so I'm sure when he's ready we'll see each other. We'll talk." She shrugged. "You know."

He pulled a piece of paper out of his pocket. "I thought you would say that. But I want you to have this anyway."

Evie took the paper with a frown. "What is it?"

"Jake's address and home telephone number. In case you change your mind. You know, I never thought you would sit back and let something good slip through your fingers."

She bristled. "What do you mean?"

"I always thought if you wanted something, or someone, you'd go after them full bore. All guns blazing." He winced. "Sorry, wrong analogy. But you get my drift."

She had to get out of there before she started blubbering. "You're assuming Jake is something I want." She bent, picked up her purse, and shoved the paper inside. "I've got to go." She kissed his cheek again. "Thanks for looking out for me. I'm loving the new contracts."

"Rehearsals start in two weeks," he said as she headed to the door. "Plus we need to think about backup singers."

Evie waved a hand over her head. "Later, Conway," and she escaped. As she waited for the elevator, she pulled out the paper with Jake's address. Sixth Street. He did say he wasn't far from Balboa Park. She could, maybe, drive by. See how he was doing.

No. That was crazy thinking. "And this girl is definitely not crazy," she said aloud as the elevator doors opened. A woman inside stifled a grin. Evie got in, her cheeks hot with embarrassment, and pushed the Lobby button with a sigh. Sometimes life was just an uphill battle, no matter what.

***

Jake dropped his keys on the counter, his duffle bag on the couch, and went straight to the shower, stripping off his suit and tossing it onto his bed. His apartment had that hot, closed-up smell, but he really needed to get the travel sweat off his body. He'd worry later about how the place smelled.

He stood under the warmth of the shower, letting the water sluice off all the pain and angst of the past month. Wondered how soon he could see Evie. God, he missed her. More than he thought possible. Had he ever been this in love before? It was like he'd found the part of him that was missing, and he got butterflies in his stomach and a thrill in his heart whenever he thought about her. Now that he was back in San Diego, he wanted her with him. Filling that empty spot.

Their phone conversations had been less than satisfactory, with both of them guarded, their speech stiff and uncomfortable. He hadn't called her in a couple of days. There'd been too much to do since Marisa had died.

Now he was home, and his obligations to the dead were done. Now it was time to claim a relationship with Evie. To start figuring out what kind of life they could forge together. Well, maybe not now, he admitted as he yawned. He needed food, beer, and sleep, plus time to think things through. Not necessarily in that order.

Done with his shower, he toweled off and pulled on a pair of jeans before going around to his windows and opening them all. He turned the ceiling fan on in the living room and lit a stick of incense in his bedroom.

He checked the clock. Just past two in the afternoon. After lunch, but who the hell cared? He punched in the number for Ciro's and ordered a pizza to be delivered. The nearly empty fridge held the most important thing, some Stone IPA. He grabbed one, poured it, and went to his balcony at the rear of the apartment.

Toward the right, he could see the towering eucalyptus trees of Balboa Park. To the left was the canyon running behind the whole street. Nothing but trees and brush and wildlife. He sat, put his feet up on the wrought-iron railing, and inhaled deeply. The air always seemed cleaner, purer here in this part of the world.

San Diego. How lucky was he to live here? Pretty damn lucky, he mused, sipping on his beer. He closed his eyes and lifted his face to the sun. He'd hear the pizza guy, as the door was directly opposite the balcony. He wondered idly where he and Evie would live. She'd talked about selling her house, but he knew how much she loved it. It was certainly in a nicer neighborhood than his apartment.

But he had money in savings. They could buy a place new to them, start over. Near the beach if that was what she wanted. He wouldn't care, as long as she was happy.

The knock came sooner than he expected. He jolted out of his daze and got to his feet, momentarily disoriented. Pizza. Right. Which meant he needed his wallet. The knock came again.

"Just a minute," he called, and went to dig his wallet out of his pants pocket. A third knock came as he was reaching for the door. He opened it, looking down at his wallet. "In a hurry today, Diego?" But he didn't smell the expected pizza. Instead, something light, floral, and totally feminine floated on the air.

His head jerked up. Evie stood there at his door, looking wonderful. Tired, hair curling every which way, she was wearing jeans and his favorite pink tee shirt and had a wary look in her eyes. Totally wonderful. He could feel the grin eating up his face and reached out to her, pulling her into his arms. "There you are. I was just dreaming of you, and there you are. It's like magic."

She had stiffened up, but he didn't let go. Just hugged her, breathed her in, pressed kisses to her hair. Finally her arms crept around his waist and with a little sigh, she hugged him back. Mumbled something against his chest. As much as he didn't want to let her go, he figured they'd better get the heavy stuff out of the way first.

So he took a step back, lifted her chin and pressed a light kiss on her lips. "I didn't hear a word of that. I've got pizza coming, and there's beer in the fridge. Come on in." He stepped to one side and watched as she stepped inside far enough for him to close the door. She jumped at the sound.

"Sorry. Percussive noises. I still get spooked." Her voice was husky and sweet and it reminded him of the first time he met her, in the moonlight on the beach.

"I understand. Beer?" Jake kept it light. No sense in letting her see how his heart ached for her right now. He shoved his wallet into his back pocket.

"Yes." She cleared her throat. "That would be nice."

"And like I said, I've got our favorite pizza coming. Ciro's." He pulled the beer out of the fridge, found another glass and poured for her.

"Thank you." She took the glass from him. Looked around. "Nice."

"You're being too kind. I call it Utility Brown," he said. "Come on out to the balcony. It's nicer out there."

She followed him out and they settled at the chairs. Jake waited for her to start talking, but instead her gaze flitted from the trees to the hillside and back again. He smiled. He didn't mind opening the conversation.

"Thank you for coming by. I wasn't sure if you had the address. Not that I was here until today." He shook his head. "It's been a rough month."

Her gaze flew to him. "You're okay?"

"I'm fine." He studied his beer for a moment before meeting her anxious eyes. "Marisa died a week ago." He lifted his glass. "May she rest in peace."

Evie exhaled and tapped her glass to his. "I'm so sorry. How are you?"

Jake rubbed his face. "Tired. She hadn't changed her life insurance, or her will. I was still named as executor, so I had some cleanup to do."

"You should have told me. Not that our conversations were at all comfortable." She shrugged, took a sip of beer.

"I didn't think that talking about our relationship over the phone was a good idea. I much prefer having you within touching distance," he added. "But talking to you became the highlight of my life. Even though they were stilted, uncomfortable conversations."

"God, I missed you," she admitted, running a finger around the rim of her glass. "You were the only family Marisa had, I take it."

"Yes." Jake studied her. "After we divorced, apparently she couldn't get a job on another police force. She went to Los Angeles to be with some guy, but he was bad news. She's been mostly alone. She had no one, Evie."

Tears rolled down her cheeks, but Jake stayed on his side of the table. Evie nodded and wiped her face.

"That's sad."

"Yeah. One of the few coherent times she had, Marisa begged me to stay with her. She didn't want to die alone. So I promised that I would."

"You're a good man." Evie's eyes widened as she thought. "This means the charges against Ted will include murder."

"Another reason I stayed behind. I was able to put everything we'd collected in front of the Los Angeles cops. They've been in touch with Scottsdale and Las Vegas police. I did some of the footwork for them, but now it's all theirs. I heard you were deposed last week?"

"Yeah. That means it's all behind us, until the trial. *If* there is a trial." Evie put her beer down on the table between them. "What now? Between you and me, I mean. I'm going on tour in a couple of months. So. Do you want to extend this—thing we have—until then?"

Tension stretched between them. Evie held herself so tightly, as if she'd shatter with the wrong answer. Still, he had to make her understand.

"No. I don't want to be lovers for a couple of months."

Shock filled Evie's eyes and she turned away. "Oh—okay. I understand."

"No, you don't understand. Not at all." Jake stood and surveyed the tiny balcony. He'd look like a fool, but better to do the thing properly.

His doorbell rang, along with Diego's signature double knock. Jake sighed. "This time it is the pizza. Don't move; I'll be right back."

Jake grabbed the pizza from Diego and shoved thirty bucks in the man's hand. "Sorry. Busy. Bye." He shut the door in Diego's face, dropped the pizza on the coffee table, and returned to the balcony.

She hadn't moved. She still held that frozen position turned away from him.

"This is the worst place possible. Well, no, I'm sure if I tried I could find places that are worse," he admitted, moving his chair into the living room. "Still, I can't wait for the right place or the right time. Grab our beers, Evie, would you?"

Surprised, she picked up both beers, and watched as he moved the table into the living room.

He smiled, took the beers from her and set them down on the table behind them, then knelt on one knee in front of her on the tiny balcony. "I'd planned on being fully dressed. I'd planned on having champagne. But now that I think about it, here, on this balcony, in the middle of the afternoon, is the best possible place.

"Evie Marcherand, will you do me the very great honor of becoming my wife?"

She stared at him. Blinked. She pushed her hair out of her eyes. "Why?"

He grinned. "A fair question. Mind if I sit now? One knee isn't comfortable." At her nod, he sat at her feet and reached for her hand. "Why do I want to marry you? Because I can't see my future without you in it, that's why. Because you are the first thing I think of when I wake up and the last thing before I sleep. Because you hold my heart, and you have almost from the very first time we met, there on the beach in the moonlight. And, finally, because I've been without you for a month and I don't want to be without you for that long ever again."

"How are you planning on fixing that? We both work. I'll be going on the road and your work is here."

"I've been considering the possibility of closing up shop for a while now. Which is why I had planned on going to Spain and France. Oh, and I forgot something. Hang on a minute," and Jake scrambled to his feet. He went into the living room and rummaged in his duffle bag. Came out again, and handed her a fairly big box. "For you. Open it." He sat at her feet again.

She looked at it, then at him, one eyebrow raised. "This isn't a ring box," she said.

He laughed. "Go on. Open it."

She lifted the lid on the box, and her face cleared. She grinned at him. "You got me a cell phone. Is there a two-year contract on it?"

"Nope. Not two years, not two months. That phone is yours on one condition, and that's if you're willing to keep me for a lifetime contract."

Evie let the phone rest in her lap. "You just want to take care of me. Because I'm like Marisa, and have no one."

Surprised, Jake wrapped his arms around his knees. "Well, that's one way of looking at it, but I wouldn't say it's the right way. You are strong. If I had thought you couldn't live without someone taking care of you, do you really think I'd have spent the time at Marisa's side?"

"As she lay dying? Yeah, I do." Evie's chin went up.

"Okay, how about this? If I thought you couldn't take care of yourself, wouldn't I have forced my sisters on you to make sure you were happy and fed and that your arm healed nicely? I heard about your arm through a police report," he added.

Evie ran both hands through her hair. "Tell me what happened that night."

"Let's start from when you gave me a heart attack by sitting up on the stage and becoming a prime target for Ted." He gazed into her beautiful eyes, watched as she filtered back through the memories to that one.

"Yeah, okay. Then what?"

"You were magnificent. Brave. Got him talking, which enabled a cop to come in from behind without him hearing. Enabled me to get into place. Enabled a whole lot of people to leave the room safely."

"Then he started shooting," she said, and her face went white.

"Then he started shooting. He sprayed the audience, just above waist level. Me and the other cop had to hit the floor to avoid being hit. Then the gun kept going and got Brad."

He took a breath. "After the cops grabbed Ted, I checked for you, and you were fine; Conway was beside you, and you were both kneeling over Brad. There was pandemonium in the room. I went to Marisa, and she had a chest wound. We didn't know how bad it was, but she was the worst off and so scared. She begged me not to leave her."

Evie took a deep breath and smiled. "And you couldn't turn her down."

"But I came to you, hugged you, kissed you. And I'm here now, and even if you don't want to be my wife, I want to be a part of your life. I'll work for free as your personal bodyguard and sex slave."

"Sex slave?"

"I'll work for pizza and sex." He grinned up at her. "What do you say?"

She leaned forward and gave him her mouth. As they kissed, Jake felt most of his weariness drop away. Here she was, the love of his life. Someday maybe they'd even get hitched.

Evie pulled away. Eyed his bare chest. "You're decidedly less stuffy than you were five weeks ago."

He grinned. "Pizza?"

She nodded and her eyes shone with joy. "Pizza, beer, sex, and a long, lovely time on the road. Together. It seems that, while I am perfectly able to stand on my own two feet and take care of myself, I have become hopelessly addicted to having you in my life."

Jake stood, pulled her to her feet, and kissed her again. "Come on. Pizza. Beer. You and me. Marriage, eventually. Yes?"

Evie sent him a searching look. "What about France and Spain?"

He brushed the hair out of her eyes. "I thought we could go there together, if you're okay with that. So, what do you say?"

Evie let out a happy squeal and hugged him tightly, then made him a happy man.

"Yes. Yes. A thousand times yes."

ABOUT THE AUTHOR

Christine Ashworth grew up listening to the sound of her father's manual typewriter as he wrote and sold over 300 novels. Now, to her delight, she's the one writing novels. But as her dad is still writing away, she's got some major catching up to do.

Christine is a romantic from way back, having first picked up Harlequin romances at the age of twelve, then falling in love with bigger books when she swiped her mother's copy of Rosemary Rogers' Sweet Savage Love. She's happily married to an actor/dancer/guitarist/hippy, has two sons, and tends her garden and her family in Southern California. You can read about her cooking, gardening, and wine picks at her website at http://christine-ashworth.com.

Find Christine here:

website: http://christine-ashworth.com
Twitter: https://twitter.com/CCAshworth
FB: https://www.facebook.com/ChristineAshworthAuthor

Did you enjoy this book? Drop us a line and say so! We love to hear from readers, and so do our authors. To connect, visit www.boroughspublishinggroup.com online, send comments directly to info@boroughspublishinggroup.com, or friend us on Facebook and Twitter. And be sure to check back regularly for contests and new releases in your favorite subgenres of romance!

Are you an aspiring writer? Check out www.boroughspublishinggroup.com/submit and see if we can help you make your dreams come true.

www.ingramcontent.com/pod-product-compliance
Lightning Source LLC
Chambersburg PA
CBHW060818120626
46557CB00001B/273